A LOVER'S DEBT

RAMSEY TESANO IV

BY

ALTONYA WASHINGTON

A LOVER'S DEBT

Copyright © 2013 by AlTonya Washington

ISBN: 9780615896366

Printed In USA by CreateSpace (www.createspace.com)

Cover Artwork Courtesy of iStockphoto (www.istockphoto.com)

A Lover's Debt

To My Insatiable Readers! You Guys Are The Best!

A Lover's Debt

~FIRST PROLOGUE~

The chilly breeze from the slamming door shut out the sounds of laughter and conversation and created a fresh dusting of goose bumps along her smooth, unblemished dark skin. The silken pearl material of the evening gown was the perfect enhancement, providing her with an unnecessary but undeniably vibrant appeal.

"I told you to be sure."

She heard his voice seconds after the door closed and withstood another chill as his words thundered against her earlobe even though he hadn't yelled or scarcely spoken above his normal tone.

"You knew what it would cost you to follow me," he continued.

"You can't expect me not to feel," she spat, turning her head but not giving him the full benefit of her gaze. "Was I just supposed to shut off my emotions?"

"Do what you will with your emotions."

She felt him at her side then, murmuring the words which held an even chillier frequency when they eased into her ear.

"I only care that you shut down your mouth."

Turning then, she faced him fully. "How can you be so cold?"

"I never lied to you, Sugar." The sweet endearment and the softness of voice, never quite penetrated the hardness of his gaze. "I never gave you any reason to think that situation meant anything to me."

"Situation?"

"You knew what you were walking away from when you agreed to become part of my world."

She looked past his shoulder toward the door where the party still raged and entertained the guests of 'his world'. "What you said out there was cruel," her lashes fluttered on the memory but she would not close her eyes. "Everyone will know what I did and they'll think-"

"Who gives a fuck?" He interjected on an ill-humored hiss. "Them? Not even a little bit. Every last one of 'em's got skeletons far fouler and much older than any we could claim. Trust me," his upper lip curled into a smile that could claim neither amusement nor fondness.

"If you want the truth, they probably feel better about you now, knowing you had the balls to do something like that."

Horror bloomed in her eyes and was equally proportioned to the horror echoed in her gasp. "How could you say this?" Her question was practically swallowed by the richness of his laughter.

"*This* is who I am," the declaration held no shred of laughter when he bent to look directly into her eyes. "You'd do best to accept it, else it may surprise you terribly to discover that I'm much worse than you've already found me to be." The unreadable smile returned and curiosity held it then. "I think you've already gotten a whiff of that though, haven't you? You know what my business is-"

"And it's sick!"

He didn't seem to mind her outburst. "Sick, hmm? But it didn't cause you to turn away from the benefits, did it?" His gaze was hooded and slid down to study the diamond linked through a silver chain at her neck- a diamond of equal size sat on a band snug around her pinkie finger.

He cupped his hand beneath the chain so that the fat gem rested on his palm. "This," he bounced the diamond, "was a gift and I don't give gifts often. You see baby, everyone earns their stay here. *Everyone.*"

Her eyes widened, gleaming with a knowing intensity as fear sparkled within the translucent depths. "You really would have..." She murmured. Until that moment, she had never truly believed that he would subject his own to such a fate.

"Why not?!" His bellow, mixed with a roar of laughter. Then; like the flipping of a switch, his smile clouded. The laughter in his eyes turned into a black smolder.

"Why?" He repeated, inclining his head at a curious set. "Because there's blood between us? A union between a whore and her john?"

Again, she gasped raising a hand to her cheek as though his words had been a physical blow.

"I'm sorry, sweet," as if to console, he moved closer to pat her cheek like she was a child he wanted to pacify. "But it's a good practice to never forget where we come from, else we risk going back there. Isn't that right?" He waited for her nod, nodding as well to prod her along. Then he was applying a kiss to her forehead and offering his arm to escort her back out to the party and their guests.

The door closed with a tiny click behind the elegantly attired couple. Only then was there a stir near the heavy midnight blue drapes that ran the impressive length of the furthermost wall of the study.

The young woman who emerged from behind the finely crafted material held an expression of curiosity mingled with a trace of humor.

"Now I wonder what *that* was about?" She asked herself.

~SECOND PROLOGUE~

Holly Springs, North Carolina- 5 years ago~

"Don't be upset with Taurus."

"I could never be upset with Taurus. What lie did you run down to make him give you my number, Daddy?" Dena Ramsey smiled at the sound of her father's shudder when it rushed through the phone line.

Apparently using the sighing technique to draw on the forces of calm, Houston Ramsey gulped in several more drags of air before he continued.

"Can't a father check in on his daughter?" He asked.

"Sure. Only you aren't that father and I haven't been that daughter in a long time."

"Honey, I know we've had our differences-"

"Differences?" She laughed the word but the gesture claimed harshness instead of amusement. "Now *that's* a new way of describing it."

"I need you to listen-"

"I've listened all I plan to."

"Sweetheart don't hang up. Please I- I'm begging you."

"What do you want, Dad?"

"I'm tired of our distance, Honey." He expelled another sigh. "I want you to remember that you have a family who loves you."

"I know that. I also know that there are two kinds of love- the unconditional kind and the kind with strings. I cut our strings a long time ago."

"Dena-"

"Don't call me again," she slammed down the phone in her father's ear.

~CHAPTER ONE~

Her legs were freezing. Dena had never cared for the black leather furniture Carlos had selected for the den but; as she'd allowed him one room in their new home other than his study to express his interior decorating skills, she'd had no choice but to grin, bear and spend as little time in the purely masculine space as possible.

So what the hell was she doing in there? She knew she was there without even opening her eyes. She needed only to turn her face into one of the brown suede pillows that dotted the length of the sofa and carried the crisp spicy fragrance of his cologne and naturally evocative scent. The smell of him filled her nostrils and provided welcoming warmth against the chill brought on by the leather.

She frowned, wanting very much to open her eyes and only then discovering that it pained her to do so. Her frown triggered an ache and she winced to acknowledge the sensation that streamed all the way to her jaw.

Pain stirred on the opposite side of her face and that, she pinpointed as a slap. The realization brought the events of the last ten minutes back to the surface of her memory. At that point, opening her eyes was the last thing she wanted to do.

Unfortunately for Dena, her current houseguests weren't in favor of letting their hostess doze away the afternoon especially when they'd paid a visit specifically to see her. The slaps were a clear effort to rouse her from the unconscious state rendered from the force of Maeva Leer's powerful blow which had made contact almost the instant Dena had pulled open her front door.

"Come, come now Denny. Surely five minutes is long enough to nap and we've got so much to chat about."

Still, Dena resisted wincing then in an effort to keep her eyes closed against the terror waiting on the other side of her lids. The pain brought on by the wincing was a welcomed reaction as opposed to looking into the faces of her former associates. She caught a whiff of Evangela Leer's familiar smell and could even feel tendrils of the woman's hair against her cheek when she bent close to speak against Dena's ear.

"Open your eyes, bitch or Mae's next love tap won't be nearly as sweet."

Drawing from some deep and long since visited well of courage, Dena did as she was told. Briefly, she observed the room through the heavy dusting of lashes which barely fluttered as she summoned her eyes to open. Knowing that further hesitation would result in another slap or... something equally unpleasant, she lifted her gaze. She first spied the massive fist poised just beneath her jaw and set to deliver another blow.

"There we go," Evangela's deceptively encouraging voice colored the air with a current that could invoke sensuality, humor or bone-chilling fear without shifting an octave.

Dena had hoped it would be enough to simply focus on the pronounced fist she knew to be Maeva Leer's.

Maeva made that impossible. Awkwardly, she angled her head this way and that in an effort to put her face in the line of Dena's still down-turned gaze. Maeva's maneuverings however were most successful in landing additional amounts of the woman's solid poundage across Dena's ribcage causing her to gasp for the air Maeva pushed from her lungs. Doffing the last of her hesitation then, Dena finally met the expectant gazes of her old associates.

Evangela Leer's face was so similar to her own, Dena thought making note of the woman's flawless licorice dark skin that was claimed by so many of the Ramseys. Beyond the coloring though, there were other similarities- the same rounded and delicately crafted chin, the pitch, silken hair that bounced and brushed the shoulders- it was all there. With the exception of the rounded quality of Dena's face; which gave her a beckoning baby-doll allure, Evangela's face was a perfect oval that provided her with a striking look that she used to considerable advantage.

There were the eyes- both pairs darkly entrancing- exotic some might say given their slight squint and tilted corners. Yet in the orbs so similar to her own, Dena saw what she knew others must. It was what made her cousin so formidable, what made others bend to...well whatever she would have them. In those depths, was a darkness that had nothing to do with color and everything to do with the soul. In those depths, Dena saw what she knew everyone else did when they looked into the eyes of Evangela Leer- a predator.

Given that unsettling truth, Dena didn't hold much stock in the concern flooding the woman's lovely, assessing stare. Gently, Eva brushed the back of her hand along Dena's jaw. She'd claimed a corner of the Maplewood coffee table nearest the sofa Maeva had placed Dena on after knocking her cold.

"Tsk, tsk…" Evangela gestured over the span of a few seconds. She shook her head, sending heavy tumbles of dark hair flipping about the crisp collar of her white short waist suitcoat.

"Mae really did miss you, Hon," she lamented in a tone that would have been believable were it not for the faint cocky smile tilting a corner of her mouth. "I'm afraid that love tap of hers is gonna leave a mark." She observed.

Suddenly, she abandoned the gentle stroke she made across Dena's jaw for a grip and squeeze that sent Dena twisting in pain. Meanwhile, the leather creaked and whined in response to her erratic moves.

For a time, Evangela stared. Her elegant features harbored a stoic quality and she appeared colder, virtually detached from emotion even as she looked down on the woman squirming in the discomfort she brought forth with her touch.

"Mae, it looks like we've gone and made another enemy," she crooned, seamlessly shifting into a caring mode. "Denny's sexy beast of a hubby will want our asses for marking his bitch, won't he Denny?" Evangela's tone had transitioned again. That time, a deceptive humor was reflected.

"I suppose he's entitled," Evangela shrugged, barely sending a ripple through the suitcoat when she lifted her slender shoulders and sent a wink in Dena's direction. "I definitely won't make myself hard to find. I've seen Carlos McPhereson and he can have my ass anytime."

Dena bristled, but the move was in reaction to the sound that resembled every bit of a growl. It rose from where Maeva still rested over her ribcage.

Evangela nudged Dena's shoulder then and leaned in wearing a look of sudden camaraderie. "Mae wasn't too happy to hear that you'd given your heart to another."

Maeva pulled up her big head then and Dena couldn't pretend not to see the woman gawking her way. Freakish was the appropriate description for the woman whom Dena had been wary of since the first day she'd agreed to help finance Evangela Leer's then fledgling crew.

Dena had immediately realized that she wasn't the only one unnerved by the boss's abnormally large sidekick. Nevertheless, it didn't take her long to understand that the two were a pair or that Maeva Leer had taken a distinct liking to her.

Now, the woman lay there looking up at her with the child-like grin spread across an unexpectedly lovely face. A face enhanced by a wicked scar that ran from the lower half of her cheek to beneath her ear and around her nape.

Dena felt the full weight of dread settle deep in her belly. In the bad old days, Maeva's overt attraction had been an annoyance which she'd successfully evaded. Now, with too many betrayals and the evasion of her accomplices for a number of years, Evangela may not be of a mind to leash her monster.

"You'll have to excuse Mae, Denny," Evangela selected that moment to intervene. "The crew's suffered a few blows lately but I'm sure you already heard about those gruesome fireworks in Scotland."

Dena schooled her reaction a little too late.

Evangela smiled. "I'm sure you were hoping that we'd all gone up in flames or…gone the way of the dog, I should say. Sorry. We only suffered two casualties; Rain and Casper. Poor Mae took a tumble," Evangela stroked a finger along the line of Maeva's wicked scar. "I think it's safe to say she emerged the victor over the Scotsman's beasts. Lula broke her arm. Saffron's got some nasty gashes on hers. Santi's got a broken leg. My back took somewhat of a beating and that's all the news that's fit to print."

She slapped her hands to her thighs.

"Thankfully, Saf's arm hasn't stopped her from cracking databases and scouring the web." Evangela continued, waving her hand to urge Maeva to let Dena sit up.

Dena sucked in a welcomed breath when the weight lifted. Mae took the liberty of straightening Dena's outfit, tugging at the hem of her stylish crimson coat dress only after giving Dena's thigh a few squeezes.

"I tell you that Saf is a pure whiz." Evangela strolled the den, while praising her tech geek Saffron Manoa. "If it weren't for her obsession with the web, who knows when we'd have figured out that our former host Captain Perjas- the man you know as Jasper Stone was exchanging vows in Mozambique with his delicious son-in-law and plump baby girl there to witness all the joy." Evangela pivoted on the heel of a chic gray pump and clasped her hands in a show of glee.

"Those pesky online newspapers, you just never know when their photographers are gonna pop up."

"That's a lie," Dena grated out, though she could see in Evangela's and Maeva's expressions that it was all truth. "What do you want?" she managed.

Dena barely had the time to blink before Evangela had made the swift trip back to the coffeetable where she perched on the edge and then snatched Dena's bruised jaw into another painful grip.

"I want much," Evangela's gaze was black with deadly menace. "We've got so much time to make up for, love. You've missed out on a lot of payments, jobs and we won't get into all the private time Mae missed out on with you." She eased her hold on Dena's jaw. "Now we can either get on with the business or I can let Mae enjoy some of the pleasure I never let her indulge in before."

"No," Dena regretted the shaky response the moment it shuddered past her lips.

Evangela's laughter was full and held a contagious element. She let go of Dena's jaw in order to reach over and pat Maeva's knee when the woman proffered another lethal growl in response to Dena's sleight.

"There, there Hon," Evangela rounded out the knee pat with a rub to one of Maeva's wide muscular thighs. "We've surprised our hostess with such an unexpected visit. I'm sure she'll relax before our chat ends," her gaze shifted back to Dena. "Otherwise, we may need to break for a little one on one time to loosen her up before we continue. What'll it be, Denny?"

Dena couldn't reply, so Evangela took her incessant shaking as a show of compliance. "It's not so bad, Denny. In spite of the shameful way you've treated us, all will be forgiven as soon as you handle this final task."

Assuming the worst, Dena shook her head in reaction to the giant looming nearby. More indulgent laughter emerged from Evangela.

"Calm down, Denny it's not what you're thinking." Evangela's smile merely broadened when Dena looked her way and blinked as if just realizing a second more horrible fate.

"And we're not in the murder business anymore either," she soothed and then added a flip shrug, "Well... we are but we make enough now to uh... what's that term— 'farm out' yes! Yes we now assign those dirty jobs to the grunts who work for us."

Suddenly Evangela clapped her hands then and gave them a wave. "Maeva let Denny sit up better and get comfy." She instructed while resuming her spot on the table. "Despite all that 'farming out' stuff," she curved her middle and index fingers to quote the phrase, "there're still certain tasks we like to handle ourselves and this particular one will require your involvement." The encouraging tone of Evangela's voice vanished then along with the easy smile she'd sported.

"It'd be in your best interest to comply, Den. It'd be such a shame for sexy 'Los to come home and have the sounds of his wife being fucked by another woman to be the last things he hears before I put a bullet in his pretty head."

"Now," she rubbed her palms and then curved her hands over the edge of the coffeetable. Her voice was again soft and non-threatening. "I'd like to meet our beautiful, full-figured cousin and you're the only one who can get me close enough to arrange such a meeting."

"Belle?" Dena felt her courage reserves springing to life. "What the hell do you want with her? She's got nothing to do with whatever her father-"

"Does that sounds like compliance to you, Mae?" Eva's gaze narrowed towards her associate. "I really want to get this done quickly...what do you think'll do that best? Pleasure? Pain?"

Maeva straightened on the sofa. Evangela's question awakened a feral grin that mimicked a wildness ablaze in the strange burgundy tinged stare courtesy of her color-enhanced contacts. Needing no further encouragement, Mae launched into action. Her backhand slap sent a thick spray of Dena's blood landing against one of the leather cushions.

***

"The hell I will!"

Michaela Ramsey bolted from her perch on her husband's desk, the folds of her lounging robe fluttered gracefully behind her.

18

Quest Ramsey followed the outburst with a groan. Rearing back in his chair, he massaged his brow and accepted that not even the beckoning fragrance of Mick's perfume would be successful in cooling the heat of his usually slow temper. Admirably, he summoned every ounce of restraint yet in his possession to maintain a soft voice and try to get his wife to see reason.

"Not in the mood," Mick huffed at the suggestion. "All 'seeing reason' will do is keep me quiet while you and the *boys* handle it. Meanwhile, we're kept in the dark as usual until you guys see fit to dribble out a little bit of info." Momentarily, she gave thought to the tremendous secret that she and 'the girls' were keeping from the guys just then.

"And just where the hell is that coming from?" Quest ceased massaging his brow and stood.

"Oh baby," Mick softened her tone but in no way attempted to mask her sarcasm. "*That* is coming from every instance of you all withholding information for *our* protection. That's not gonna work this time. It's time for all the shit to hit the fan and tell everybody to grab a shovel."

"Belle's pregnant or have you forgotten? She doesn't need-"

"Why do men always equate pregnancy with meaning that a woman is fragile? Do any of you have a clue of how much strength it takes to carry and birth a child?"

"Christ," Quest let go of a few tethers restraining his temper. "Don't stand there and play clueless with me, Mick. You know damn well what I'm saying."

"*I* know that you want me to buy into this protection gimmick you've turned into a personality trait."

Quest staggered back a bit as if she had physically pushed him. Michaela took pity at his reaction. Bowing her

19

head, she inhaled a few breaths and waited for a grain of calm to settle.

"Sweetie, Nile and Dena deserve to have that man sit down before them and answer for the hell he dropped into their lives. They deserve that every bit as much as Fernando, Hill and Kraven deserve to confront him."

Quest returned to massaging his brow.

"Don't you think they at least deserve to know *why* he did it?" Mick clasped her hands to her chest. "Why did he involve himself in a business like this? What, if anything, does he plan to do to make it right? They deserve to hear him apologize-not that it would mean anything... Baby I'm just trying to get you to see that even the smallest gesture has merit here."

Quest took a seat on the edge of his desk and Mick joined him there seconds later.

"I'm sorry," she nuzzled a kiss into his flawless dark chocolate cheek and gave a cautious smile. "I really don't mean to make this complicated."

"Save it," his left-dimpled smile emerged when he shifted a knowing look in her direction. "You're not a bit sorry and I don't fault you for it."

Mick straightened a bit. "You don't?"

Quest toyed with one of the embroidered sleeves on Michaela's lounger. "All the secrets in my family...we hold onto 'em like gold and they've almost destroyed us." He smirked and gave a self-deprecating shrug.

"I won't apologize for my 'personality trait'," he said, "Dena's had a front row seat to the shit my uncles were a part of and what good did it do for her to be exposed to that."

Mick scooted closer, squeezing his arm between both her hands. "Baby don't you think she deserves to see the man who was at the helm of it all?"

"Let's at least wait to discuss it until after this trip," he said referring to a sudden couple's getaway they were being treated to courtesy of his sister-in-law Tykira Ramsey. "Besides, we really don't know if he's at the helm, do we?"

"We know he's one of the top dogs," Mick argued. "There're a lot of answers still out for the count Quest. If the man is really serious about being a part of Belle's life, then maybe he'll be willing to share them."

***

"Again I ask, what the hell do you want with Sabella?" Dena was stunned to discover that her well of courage was deeper than she thought. Maeva's blood-drawing blow hadn't caused her to revert into a shell of fear as it very well should have. "Answer me," she hissed and then spat a lingering stream of blood.

Evangela began to laugh wildly as though she were being tickled. "There's that fire! Hell, I knew you still had it!" She gave a single resounding clap. "I always knew you'd fit right into our little troupe, Den. You're more like us that you've ever wanted to admit."

"Bullshit. What do you want her for?" Dena repeated through clenched teeth as she struggled to dismiss the pain radiating through her jaw.

"Think about it, Denny. Do you think Captain P will just agree to a meeting if I ask for one?"

"He would before he'd tolerate you sharing breathing space with Belle."

"That may be true," Evangela stroked a perfectly manicured index nail down her licorice dark cheek and sighed. "True...but the trouble is that there would be no motivation for him to tell me what I want to know once we have our little sit down. Now with S*abella* in my possession," she gave a delighted shiver, "He's got more incentive to cooperate."

"Monster," Dena watched the woman through a narrowed and spiteful stare. "There's no way I'd be able to do that even if I wanted to- which I don't! And besides all that, her husband won't even let her out of his sight."

"I see your point," Evangela spoke the words and nodded though it was obvious the obstacle was of little disappointment. "It's true that most expectant fathers are protective that way…"

Dena gasped at the woman's elated smile. "What do you know?"

"Ah…that news pic of the happy family revealed much." Evangela left the coffeetable and began another stroll about the den. "I know quite a bit more besides- Quay and Ty's twins- girls, yes? I've got twin girls of my own," Her gaze took on something…absent before she snapped to. "They aren't mine I-I'm their aunt but one day…who knows…"

Dena had zoned off amidst Evangela's uncharacteristic rambling, her distress then was evident. Her tormentor smiled.

"Don't be upset, Denny." Evangela crooned. "I only need Belle to be there. I don't want her life or the life of her child."

"You expect me to believe that tripe?" Dena put the back of her hand against her mouth where she'd felt a trickle of blood beginning to ooze.

"That would depend on whether or not you keep your word." Evangela retraced her steps to the sofa. "Screw with us, Den and we'll have to take things into our own hands and see that's where things tend to get messy."

"What the hell do you think Jasper Stone can tell you?" Dena shook her head in wonder.

"So you're curious about that?" Evangela shrugged, looking as though she approved. "That's showing the spirit of teamwork. I like it and to answer your question, I'm interested in what he can tell me of the whereabouts of a certain research park."

"Research?" Dena queried, receiving another of Evangela's delighted smiles. "But you already know where the island is?"

Evangela's smile then bordered on exhilaration. She was then standing close enough to tap her finger to the tip of Dena's nose.

"Right you are, Den and we'd be all set without ever having to involve our lovely cousin in all this nasty business but sadly the facility I'm searching for isn't on the island I know and loathe." She took a seat next to Dena on the arm of the chair. "What happened there was merely a means to an end- a profitable means and important in its own right, but there was more afoot you know?"

"Such as?"

"Oh…there's that curiosity again," Evangela gave a delighted shiver and tapped Dena's nose once more. "No can do, Den. I'm afraid I can't spill *all* the goods for you to share with that team of investigators we call a family. Besides," she gave a sigh and pushed off the sofa's arm, "the magnificent Mr. McPhereson will be home soon." She stooped to peer closer at Dena. "Now you wouldn't be trying to let him catch us here, would you?"

Dena only raised a brow, a clear indicator that the thought was highly appealing. Evangela straightened.

"Suffice it to say that there's something in this for all of us." Seamlessly, she shifted gears from secretive to concern. "By the way, Den how are the headaches? Still having them along with those ugly dreams?"

Stunned surprise mingled in along with the courage Dena had been celebrating. The leather creaked beneath her when she fidgeted on the chair. She pressed back, plastering herself against the sofa as if somehow the move would protect her from enduring more of what Evangela's inquiry made her remember. The leather was no longer cool next to her skin, but hot as sweat began to bead and absorb into the back of her dress.

"It's alright, Denny. You don't have to answer that one. Just keep in mind that the facility in question produces a lot of wonderful things. Among them; the only thing that ever triumphed over that nasty combo of yours," Again, Evangela stooped to peer more closely at Dena.

"Remember Re-Gen, Denny?" She saw Dena's eyes widen and smiled.

"Go get the car, Mae." Evangela voiced the order without looking the woman's way and sounding every bit the boss speaking to a subordinate.

Despite the fact that Maeva significantly outweighed her boss, she did as Evangela bid without question or hesitation.

"Get this done, Dena." Evangela instructed once they were alone. "It'll go much easier for you to take sugar from us instead of shit and if that *still* isn't enough to set your ass in motion, consider the love of your life discovering all the shameful things you did *for* me, *with* others and *to* yourself during the course of our acquaintance all those years ago and then see what he thinks of his little innocent then."

With that, Evangela smoothed non-existent wrinkles from her suit and dropped a kiss to Dena's forehead on her way past. Her exit was marked only by the click of the front door lock.

~CHAPTER TWO~

"Can I help you?"

Tamara Keene successfully stifled her shriek, but she wasn't as victorious in masking the surprise in her expression or manner when she brought a hand to where the pulse beat ferociously at the base of her throat.

The man who had stirred her surprise watched her intently and Tamara wondered at how long he'd been there. She hadn't even heard him approach. Surely, it wasn't easy for a man his size to muffle his footsteps, she thought. Then again, she *had* been beating on the front door like a wild woman for the past seven minutes.

Her heart completed a backwards flip to the roof of her mouth. The reaction didn't render her speechless as she should have been staring up at the giant who glowered down at her.

"I'm sorry is- do you live here?" She asked.

Carlos McPhereson gave the woman a measured glare. "Who are you?"

"I-" The books Tamara Keene had been successfully cradling in the crook of her arm picked that moment to threaten a tumble onto the wide brick porch. She caught them just in time, clutching them to her chest while struggling to slow her breathing.

"I'm sorry, I- Tamara. Tamara Keene. I have an appointment with Dena Ramsey."

"McPhereson."

The abrupt correction caused Tamara to jump.

"What's your appointment with my wife for?"

Tamara secured her hold on the books against her chest and fumbled around in a pocket on the linen eggshell jacket she sported. "I'm a florist," she produced a card.

"Right…" Carlos studied the card the woman handed him. "She did say she had an appointment at…" he purposely trailed away, waiting for the florist to supply him the missing information.

Tamara Keene however had gotten lost in studying the honey-toned specimen whose fierce demeanor only emphasized the appeal of his divinely constructed features. And his eyes… she felt herself jump again when he spoke her name.

"Time?" He prompted.

"Oh uh-yes, yes I was to meet with her," Tamara paused to check her watch. "Twenty minutes ago," nervously she tucked a lock of silky blonde behind an ear and worked up a smile. "Normally I wouldn't stand around beating down someone's door, but when the Ramseys call…"

"Right," Carlos rolled his eyes and pocketed the florist's card.

"The women who left said she was in there and taking visitors."

Inclining his head at the revelation, Carlos smoothly invaded more of Tamara Keene's space with his considerable frame. "What women?"

"Um," Tamara blinked owlishly for several moments not quite sure whether what she'd said had stirred mere curiosity or a more dangerous element. "One was dark, pretty and tall. Uh-the other wasn't quite so- so dark, but tall, very tall- big, excessively big at first I-I thought she was a man."

Carlos murmured something indecipherable. He made an instinctive reach for one of the three weapons that adorned his body whenever he left the house. He stopped himself before freeing one of the deadly items, recalling the florist. She'd already noticed the holster he wore and was looking more wary with each ticking second.

"Thank you for your patience, Ms. Keene." His captivating pale green stare narrowed in tandem with his faint smile. "I'll find out what the issue is and have my wife get in touch soon for another meeting."

His tone left no room for disagreement while he escorted the woman to the midnight blue Camry parked before his GMC. He ushered her into the car, shut the door and waited for her to start the ignition and put the vehicle in drive. When she'd gone, he spanned the wide steps to the front door in a few long strides.

He released the silver tab securing the flap over the gun from the holster beneath his left arm. Still, he hesitated when his hand folded over the front door lever. He wanted to convince himself that; as usual, he was overreacting. He was always so ready to confront a battle when there was only a party to be had.

In his own defense, he had every right to expect the worst. Things were far from settled in the mishmash of drama, betrayal and danger that weaved into the daily lives of the Ramsey- and now Tesano- clans. While Dena was free to enjoy her friends and family until she was content, Carlos knew of only one 'big woman' who could be mistaken for a man that might have cause to pay a visit to his wife.

Hand still at rest beneath his arm, he twisted the lever with his free hand while setting his shoulder to the door. Cautiously, he leaned into it while the heavy pine slab gave.

"Hate it when I'm right," he murmured, eyeing the mess he encountered following a look into the den just off from the foyer. Fingers flexing on the butt of the gun, he continued the journey deeper into his home.

A quick scan of the lower level turned up no sign of Dena. He'd decided against calling out to her. There was no need- she was there, that much he sensed. He set the front door locks and then ascended the rich, red-wine carpeted staircase. The gun, he carried parallel to his thigh aiming it toward the floor as he made his way stealthily along the stairs, pausing intermittently to check out every room he passed.

Cocking his head as he lowered it, Carlos stilled for a moment breathing deep to take in the scent his nostrils had detected. He followed the familiar fragrance and; had only taken two steps into the bedroom's sunken living area, when unexpected force unsteadied his stance. He would have recovered quickly were it not for the kick to the shin that sent him down to one knee. The gun was knocked clear of his grip.

The attacker punished him with another kick, that time to the small of his back sending him to the floor. Carlos braced a hand to the carpet, refusing to be taken completely down. He made a sudden pivot that brought him face to face with his opponent.

"D?" He scarcely had time to register what; until then, would have seemed impossible.

Dena gave her husband no time to add further detail to his inquiry. One of her small bare feet landed a perfectly executed blow to the center of his broad chest. That move; along with the added pressure when she straddled his waist, finally sent Carlos to his back.

Later, he would ask himself how much the mere shock of the attack had to do with his defeat. Expression equal parts awe and bewilderment, Carlos watched Dena dismantle his weapon. Parts of the gun were thudding to the floor even as she suddenly gripped her head. Shaking frantically then, she cried out and squeezed her eyes shut before landing in an unconscious sprawl atop her husband.

***

Vilanculos, Mozambique~

"Am I still in the doghouse?" Isak 'Pike' Tesano settled in behind his wife on the lounge she occupied along the terrace outside their bedroom suite. Sabella Ramsey Tesano lifted her arms just slightly to give Pike room to ease his arms about her waist and settle his hands to her belly where their unborn child slumbered beneath the folds of her lavender and navy lounge dress.

"I didn't realize I ever sent you there," Belle coolly replied to his query. "Anyway, you're good as long as you keep your promise that we can join everybody on Ty's holiday trip so I can see Fernando."

"I thought maybe we could skip that and just visit everybody in Seattle closer to Christmas?" Pike suggested.

Belle was already shaking her head. "You're pushing it," she warned.

Smiling more contentedly then, Pike eased his gorgeous dark copper-toned face to rest at the crook of her neck. "So I'm not in the doghouse-"

"Yet."

"Yet…but you *have* been giving me the silent treatment."

Belle made herself more comfortable against the expanse of his chest, taking solace in the welcoming strength of his solid frame. "You know we haven't been doing much that's required a lot of talking."

"Hmm…" Pike seemed to consider her point while beginning a slow caress using his nose to smooth the wisps of chestnut brown hair that had fallen from its upsweep to brush her nape. "If you want the truth, that's actually the only time you *haven't* been giving me the silent treatment."

"Stop!" Belle dissolved into laughter then, nudging her husband's ribs with her elbow.

"Hey?" Gently, he turned her to face him on the chaise that lent a splendid vantage point to observe the sunny, colorful skies of Vilanculos near dusk.

Belle acknowledged his seriousness when he merely watched her. She patted his cheek and followed the move with a sweet kiss to his mouth. "I really can't think of wanting you in the doghouse when you're doing such amazing things. Bringing me here and then agreeing to the holiday trip…" she took a moment to take in their surroundings.

"Do you know how much it meant to watch my parents get married?"

Pike gave a playful wince. "Had to feel a little weird to watch your folks taking vows when one is somebody you never knew existed before a few months ago."

"Yeah," she nodded, "but weird in a happy way-not scary."

It was Pike's turn to observe the enchanting environment they'd already been a part of for well over a week. "Your father's really loved here," he made the observation cautiously. "The people treat him like a king."

Despite the pleasant warmth of the late sun, Belle shivered as if kissed then by an unexpected chill. "You noticed that too, huh?"

"Mmm… but they treat him like he's a happy king, not a scary one."

Belle laughed at his play on her words before a wave of something serious doused the gesture.

"It's not easy becoming a king, is it?" She asked.

"It's not," Pike agreed, settling back more comfortably and taking Belle with him.

"How do you think he made that happen?" She asked.

Pike tightened his embrace just a tad and only for a brief time. "I don't know, Bella." His features stiffened into a bleak mask that in no way marred the beauty of his features. Then, he was pressing his mouth to her ear.

"I love you."

She felt his mouth curve into a smile and her contentment was refueled. "You're everything to me," she returned.

Together, they enjoyed what remained of the sunset.

***

"D?" Carlos smothered Dena's upper arms in his wide grasp, tugging her limp form up over him so that he could look into her face.

"Baby?" He could barely hear his own voice above the rush of his heartbeat churning blood to his ears. Easily, he switched their positions putting Dena on the floor and placing her on her back. His uncommon stare never left her face while he searched it.

His hands smoothed her cheeks before he squeezed his eyes shut, ordering himself to calm and think. Feeling his heart rate steady then, he bent close to listen for her breathing. Unfairly lengthy lashes drifted shut over his eyes once more when he rested his head on her chest to listen for her heart rate.

The muscle pumped a steady beat. Far steadier than his own, he noted. He mouthed a thankful prayer and then put a heavy kiss into her neck before rising to his haunches. His intention was to carry her to the bed and allow her to rouse under her own steam.

With an effortless fluidity that harbored a stunning grace for someone so massive, Carlos took Dena from the floor. He waited, before laying her down to the double king set upon a raised and deeply carpeted platform in the rear of their bedroom. Preferring then to simply cradle her, he kept her an unconscious prisoner in his arms, nuzzling his face into the lush dark waves of her hair. She squirmed and he immediately set her down, situating her in the center of the bed to secure her in the shelter of his arms once he'd set fists on either side of her into the worsted fabric of the cognac brown comforter.

"D? Baby open your eyes. Honey..." he murmured the words along her jaw as his mouth grazed there on its way up to apply the same attention to the curve of her cheek.

Dena squirmed, the move a bit more pronounced then. She groaned and Carlos took note of her fists clenching where her hands rested at her sides. He waited, watching the elegant arch of her brows draw into a frown.

"Babe? It's me...open your eyes for me...it's Los," he leaned closer to speak the words into her ears before nuzzling there and applying a dry suckle to the satiny, fleshy lobe.

Dena's next squirm was more of a wrench- a violent twisting that put distance between she and Carlos. Eyes closed, she blindly lashed out, swinging clenched fists at whatever her thoughts revealed.

"D," his voice was cool-nothing out of the ordinary. Rarely, did he allow temper to triumph over his calm-not the best habit for someone in his line of work. Temper certainly had no place there, not when fear and pain were engulfing almost every part of him. Pain over what he saw her going through then- fear over what he could only imagine.

"Get off…" her voice was a low groan the two words almost slurring together as she continued to thrash on the bed.

Carlos intended to give her room to drain her need to fight, yet he kept a close vigil on the bed. Underestimating his wife's fighting style and cleverness to boot, he didn't factor in that she might make a play for his second weapon.

She did and was relieving Carlos of the firearm he kept at his hip even as she crawled to the other side of the bed. She didn't aim it, but the fact that she had possession of it at all was terrifying in and of itself.

Carlos didn't allow his surprise to undermine him that time. He was dragging Dena beneath him before she had time to reach the other side of the enormous bed. Her cry was one of pure rage as she tried to kick out at him even as he covered more of her with his considerable weight.

"Get off!" She thrashed wildly, her hair landing in a messy tangle in her lovely and furious face.

Unmindful of her raging, Carlos was more concerned about his gun which she still waved wildly above her head as she struggled to free herself.

"Bitch," she hissed when one of his hands captured both her wrists. Her two handed grip on the gun tightened before the slight pressure Carlos added to his hold sent her shrieking in pain. Her hands went weak as the weapon thudded to the flooring beneath the bed's platform.

Carlos shut down his sympathy. He knew his hold was causing her pain but also knew he wasn't exerting any bruising power. She was still whimpering though. The small pained mewling sounds streamed consistently as he put her on her back again.

"Bitch..." the curse was scarcely a murmur.

It told Carlos much. "Shh...baby shh...it's me, it's Los..."

"Get off...get off me..."

He made no other attempts to silence her. Settling alongside his wife, he held her until she drifted off into another disquieted slumber.

***

"You never complained about it before."

"I wasn't living here before."

"Is that right? I seem to recall moving- 'scuse me'- being *told* to move over half my clothes from my walk in."

"Serves you right for not having walk-ins in all the bedrooms."

"There *are* walk-ins in all the bedrooms."

"'Scuse *me, I* should've said *sit-ins* where you can watch a damn movie while selecting an outfit and then relax on a big ass sofa while you get dressed."

"I'm a big man. I deserve big things."

Contessa Warren Ramsey silenced her comeback when she felt a smile threatening to accompany it. "Don't make me laugh."

"Wouldn't think of it," Fernando Ramsey slanted his wife a wink accompanied by a sly grin. "Besides, you can't make me move a chair now in my condition."

"Bullshit," Contessa threw back allowing her laughter its escape then. "Your condition hasn't stopped you from doing anything you really want to do. So how about doin' something *I* really want you to do."

Light eyes crinkling adorably and devilishly then, Fernando caught County's waist before she'd read his intentions to capture her. "I thought I *had* been doing things you really want me to."

"Stop." She ordered, pretending to be unaffected by his fingers skirting the hem of her sleep shirt while his mouth skimmed her collarbone. "I won't change my mind about that hideous chair. My settee would look way better in that spot anyway."

"Come on, babe. It's my favorite." He murmured, his tongue skimming her collarbone then.

"I thought *I* was your favorite?" She decided to use her own brand of sultriness.

"Oh yes," Fernando cupped her bare bottom beneath the shirt.

"Ramsey…" County whined, knowing he was seconds from lifting her off her feet.

"Alright, alright," he gave in making no move to relinquish his hold. "It's nothing for us to get a divorce over…"

A chill hit County so violently then that she actually shivered. Her reaction was so jarring, that Fernando couldn't mistake it as a result from his touch. He pulled back to look at her, frowning the instant her eyes met his and skirted away.

"What the hell…?" He cupped her cheeks to prevent her from averting her face. "What's wrong with you?"

"Ramsey-"

"If you say nothing, Contessa…" he shifted his head once slowly to the left to warn off the mistake she was about to make.

"Alright! Dammit Ramsey!" Shrugging off his hold, she smoothed her hands up and down her arms to combat the chills riddling her skin. "Teasing about divorce is not the thing to do when I just almost lost you, okay?"

The tension in Fernando's broad shoulders released. He shook his head then in a sign of regret. "Jesus...babe, I'm sorry," he drew her closer then dragging his fingers through her boyishly cut hair while kissing her temple.

County felt herself relax some due in part to the fact that her husband bought her excuse. Relaxation filtered in a bit more when she reasoned; as she had many times since the Scotland trip, that she had no reason to berate herself for keeping quiet about what she and the other women had learned. After all, that particular truth was for Persephone James to share.

And what of the fact that she shot your husband? Don't you think he might like to know that? Would he think your keeping that particular truth hidden from him would be something to divorce over?

Fernando muttered a curse, feeling Contessa's shivers backbuild. "Hey?" He gave her a playful shake. "Let's make a deal. We've already broken in my chair, right?"

Agitated as she was, County couldn't resist smiling over the lusty memory. "A moment I'm not proud of," she said.

"Yeah..." Fernando grinned. "I could tell by all your screaming and moaning and 'yes Ramsey, yesses', that you were totally disgusted by it."

"Anyway..." she rolled her eyes as more animation filtered her voice.

"Anyway," Fernando drew her close again. "If the settee gives us a better...ride than my chair, I'll get rid of it by the weekend. The week," he added when her eyes narrowed. "Deal?" He took her off her feet, his destination the second floor den where County's settee presently resided.

"Deal," she murmured against his mouth happy to let Fernando clear her mind of everything.

***

The whimpering curdled deep in her throat. It was faint and would have been entirely missed were he not so close to her. Carlos raised his head to study her face- a living doll if ever there was one. He'd loved Dena Ramsey all his life. Sure the inescapable tug of her features had been the catalyst for the attraction. He *was* once a hormone induced kid, after all.

Yet, as fascinated as he was by her looks, he later realized that it was the hint of despair lying veiled beneath the glow of her pretty face that had bound him. It was the despair that had awakened the basest of all male instincts- the desire to protect.

Heat stirred in his eyes then. Simmering into a pale green with olive highlights, that stare had been known to radiate such intensity that it could drain strength from the legs of the most brutal men. Gently, Carlos brushed his fingertips across the bruise that rested just below her eye and covered the uppermost region of her cheek. The mark was easily visible against the satiny licorice of her skin which meant the blow had been given with deliberate force- considerable power.

Maeva Leer, he thought knowing it had to have been she and Evangela who'd had nerve enough to come calling that day. But why this? Again, he rubbed at the bruise. Aside from a slight puffiness courtesy of a split to one side of her bottom lip, her face carried no other blemishes.

Through his work and sideline attempts to gain whatever knowledge he could concerning other matters, Carlos had stumbled across Evangela Leer and her crew. Little was known about them and he had only recently

37

attached names to the lethal bunch. Still, none of the attacks he had linked them to- with the exception of the recent event in Scotland- had ever involved them going after women. In truth, their visit in Scotland was meant for Kraven and Fernando not Darby and Contessa.

Carlos recalled the men they had… handled previously. They were scum anyone would have celebrated being rid of. So why this- and why now? Why would they come after Dena this way? Softly, a voice reminded him that there may have been unfinished business but again he asked 'why now'?

Dena's low whimpering gained a few decibels and she began an awkward yet faint squirm beneath him. Carlos waited, deciding to let her awaken under her own power. He stifled some of his weight, but didn't completely relieve her of his bulk. Her squirm intensified and it was then that he understood that she was struggling, attempting to fight again. Her whimpers weren't whimpers at all, they were muffled screams.

Nevertheless, he waited hoping she might reveal more through her struggles. Perhaps, she'd let slip for him what her former associates wanted from her and why they wanted it from her now. The malformed screams continued, showing no signs of abating. When she at last began to pummel at his chest with her fists and order 'the bitch' to get off her, Carlos knew what- who she still had on her mind.

"D?" The rich, edgy depth of his tone held softness when he called to her. Easily, he captured her energetic fists, trapping her wrists and keeping one at either side of her head on a pillow. All the while, he settled in snug between her restless thighs once more bringing his weight down fully upon her.

"It's me," he murmured, "It's me," he continued the chant until her struggles showed signs of cooling and her breathing steadied. The deep intakes of air sent her cleavage heaving against his chest. Instantly, his thoughts shifted surging from the important matters at hand to the desire she could summon inside him with very little effort.

Momentarily, he let his forehead rest at her shoulder while grating out a vicious curse berating himself for such weakness when she was in the throes of something that horrified her. At any rate, his nearness was obviously instilling a calming effect if the consistent steadying of her breath was any proof.

"It's me, babe. It's 'Los," he smoothed his nose along her earlobe as he spoke against it.

Gradually, Dena became more lucid. She had yet to open her eyes however and still mistook her husband's weight for that of another.

"Bitch," she braced against the pressure about her wrists. Maeva Leer had gotten impossibly stronger in the last few minutes. The realization was so defeating that Dena went boneless beneath the restraining hold, accepting that she wouldn't be able to break it.

It's me, it's 'Los.

She squirmed again, the defeat she felt was being nudged aside by the slow force of… pleasure? Again, she whimpered. A whimper brought on by lust and not to preface a scream. His voice in her head, turned that whimper into a moan even as she resented its presence in her mind. It felt obscene having him there in any way while that bitch lay atop her.

It's 'Los.

Dena jerked. The voice hadn't sounded like a play of her imagination. It sounded close, so close that she could feel the words vibrating through her, filling her with spectacular warmth. Pleasure bloomed anew, splashing its syrupy branches throughout her body that was now

39

opening, arching to invite everything promised by the coaxing depth of his words.

"Not now, not now please…" It was certainly no time to be aroused, she thought continuing to resist what she most wanted.

Carlos rested his forehead lightly next to her bruised cheek. "Open your eyes."

Dena fought the command, rolling her head back and forth against the pillow beneath it.

"It's alright," he promised.

"They're here…mmm…" she moaned, walking a precarious tightrope between fear and need.

"So am I," Carlos propped fingers to his brow while he watched her. He could feel her melting in relief and terror the moment he spoke.

"Carlos…no…they…they'll hurt you…"

"Are you serious?" He couldn't help but chuckle then. "Open your eyes for me, babe."

Ill-equipped to triumph and resist anything he asked of her, Dena obeyed. Still unsteady, she bit her lip and willed herself. Her eyes filled with tears at the sight of the handsome, ruggedly crafted face before her.

"Carlos," his name eased out on her whisper.

He flashed a brilliant smile, the captivating hue of his gaze narrowing with the gesture. "Hey, Doll." He whispered.

~CHAPTER THREE~

Soothing relief was only hers to enjoy but a moment before the din of unease resurfaced to heighten her sense of foreboding.

"Shh…" Carlos could read the anxiety in her voluminous dark eyes and he knew her fears were once again getting the better of her. He also knew she didn't dare reveal to him the source of those fears.

She was trying to push herself upright on the bed. He prevented that. Having let go of her wrists, he exchanged the hold to span her waist and keep her in place.

"Are we alone?" her squirming then held a different kind of urgency.

Despite it all, Carlos laughed shortly. "Why wouldn't we be?" He asked.

Dena ceased her fidgets. Settling flat to the bed, she averted her gaze warily eyeing the absorbing artwork that graced the walls and were often a successful catalyst for serenity.

"Bad dream," she murmured, swiping hair from her clammy forehead. "How long have you been here?" She searched his eyes for a moment.

"A while."

"You should have gotten me up."

"How long were you out?" In an attempt to mask his suspicion, he feigned greater interest in stroking the hair she'd been swiping from her face. He did a fine job but the question sent her frowning as he knew it would. The fear of her earlier visitors had returned if only for a brief stay.

Discovery pooled the deep blackberry orbs of her stare and she angled it over one of Carlos' broad forearms resting on the pillow nearest her head. Her mouth gaped when she read the time on the bedside clock.

"I was supposed to meet the florist," she gasped, again she tried to sit up.

"I already saw her," Carlos flexed the hand that had been smoothing her waist. "I made an excuse for you not answering the door."

Dena collapsed back onto the litter of gold pillows at the head of the bed. "She was knocking?"

"Hell yeah she was, looking pretty put out over it too," Carlos relaxed and intentionally laid it on rather heavily. "You would've been proud of me. I made you look good, she wasn't nearly as pissed when she left."

"Oh no..." Mortification forced Dena's eyes closed.

"That must've been some nap?" Carlos wasn't ready to soothe his wife's emotions just then.

"Some nap..." Dena murmured then tried to sit again. "I should call," she was still sealed beneath Carlos who didn't budge.

"I told her you'd be in touch. You can call when we get back."

Dena forgot about the florist. "Get back?"

"Mmm hmm," he ignored her curiosity. "I know you've been goin' stir crazy in here and I'm sorry."

"Carlos-"

"No D, wait and let me say this. You were right," he fondled a lock of her hair, his light deep gaze fixated on the tendril. "I've been thick headed and there's been no reason for it."

"There was every reason for it," she countered, her voice bordering on a hiss. "After everything that happened with Fern-"

"Shh..." he gave the order against her mouth. The hand spanning her waist applied a probing massage upon her hip before gliding lower to hook one of her thighs bared by the rising of her hemline.

Dena shivered then as much from a raging case of nerves as she did from her instant and usual reaction to her husband's touch. The tip of his nose glided along her jaw, down the line of her throat and on to the swell of bosom. The fleshy mounds heaved so vivaciously that it appeared the majority of her cleavage had pushed up past the bodice that Carlos had already taken the liberty of unbuttoning.

"Carlos-" She silenced her call on the sharp intake of breath resulting from his tongue replacing his nose and taking over the job of outlining the shape of her protruding breasts.

Carlos used the tip of his tongue to nestle deep into the valley between the full, molasses dark globes. He worked his tongue in slow erotic rotations that parted the valley, allowing him more room to explore.

"Where are we going?" The question was weak, holding little volume. Clearly, she was far more interested in what was happening in the vicinity of her chest. "I need to...mmm..." she bit her lip on the sensation roused when his tongue completely disappeared between her breasts. "Carlos, I really need to fix this thing with the florist."

She was cradling his head then, her nails raking the sleek close cut cap of hair crowning his head. She arched into the suckling pressure he applied to her nipples through the fabric of her dress' bodice and bra. "Carlos-"

"Hush, I'll take you to see your florist but we've got a stop to make first."

***

Napa Valley, California~

What were the chances of such a thing happening twice in a lifetime? Pretty good, she'd wager given their business. SyBilla Ramsey closed the folders she'd been reviewing side by side and set them to the weathered wooden table arranged between two maple framed cushioned lounge chairs- one of which she occupied.

It wouldn't be the first time she'd worked a case where everyone had more facts than she did. But dammit, why did Caiphus Tesano have to be involved?

She leaned over to gather a fistful of her short curls in an effort to silence the voice that chastised her for faking disdain over working closely with the man again. When grabbing curls didn't work, she returned her energy to the case- *cases* at hand.

Was it true? Could they be connected? What happened in Scotland, what she'd seen there at the crime scene- the attack and the carnage left by Kraven DeBurgh's dogs. What she'd seen couldn't have been a coincidence. Could it?

Bill wondered if Caiphus had noticed. Would he have told her if he had? Chances were it was all lodged as far in the back of *his* mind as it was supposed to be in hers. Lamont had asked- ordered- them more than once to forget the investigation. She thought of her organization's Chief Operator Lamont Pevsner.

They had only scratched the very surface of the peculiar case so many years ago. Had Caiphus listened? *She* hadn't. Especially when it appeared she had more connections to what the case uncovered than she'd at first realized.

Again, SyBilla surveyed the photos taken at the DeBurgh estate. Her hazy stare settled on the snapshot of one of Evangela Leer's fallen crewmates.

"Why were you there?" Bill spoke to Rain Su's mauled image. She moved the shot from the evidence folder marked SCOTLAND to the one she'd pieced together for her eyes only and marked VESTIGE.

***

"So serious," Dena welcomed the air of playfulness that had stirred in her stomach while she lay there with Carlos drawing contentment from the potency of his presence. "But I really do need to get in touch with Tamara especially after missing our meeting."

"Did you really sleep through all her knocking?" His question slipped in smoothly and Dena's playful smile became a nervous one.

"I really did," was all she could manage.

Carlos nodded feeling Dena go limp beneath him as relief infused the tension which had stiffened her entire body. "It's not that big of a deal, you know?" He traced the lacy bra cups that offered teasing glimpses of the pert globes they supported. "You could've been holding the party of the year on the roof and the woman would've still forgiven you for missing that meeting."

"What's that supposed to mean?"

"Just what I said," with a shrug Carlos relieved Dena of some of his weight. "You guys can do anything

45

and get away with it- there's always someone to clean up the mess."

"Are you speaking for yourself, Mr. McPhereson?"

"Who else would I speak for?" He was in her face then, any trace of lightness long gone.

He left her on the bed and that was when Dena noticed the luggage packed and waiting by the bedroom door. At last, she pushed herself upright.

"What's up with the cases?"

"Told you we were leaving," Carlos refused her the benefit of his gaze while zipping a tan leather valise.

"And are you ready to reveal our destination?" She huffed when he provided no clarification. "You remember I'm planning my Aunt Josephine's wedding, right? I don't even think we'll have time for that romantic trip of Tykira's right now as much as I think we could use it," she tacked on when he sent her a look.

"Rest easy, babe," he tossed aside the valise. "I don't believe you'll think of this as a romantic trip."

"Why not?" Slowly, she eased off the bed taking closer notice of his tone. "Carlos, I-" She meant to insist he tell her where they were going, but stopped short when she saw the wreckage in the living area.

Carlos observed her reaction. He had intentionally left the area a mess and judged the intensity of her gaze as she looked upon the deep mocha rug that carried the proof of their earlier tussle. Dena felt the minute tingles just below the surface of her skin and she knew his eyes were following her. She didn't turn in his direction or attempt to mask her disbelief.

"What happened?" The question was hypothetical. She didn't need a response, her thoughts were focused elsewhere then. Deliberately, she moved towards the jumble of metal on the rug.

Carlos continued to observe, captivated by the sight of his wife assembling a gun with a deft calmness. Her efficiency to the task drew him toward her as deliberately as she had approached the dismantled weapon.

Dena finished the assemblage and then studied the gun like she'd never seen anything like it. Quickly, carefully, she set it to the endtable situated next to one of the sofas skirting the rug's edge. Standing then, she smoothed both hands along the front and sides of her dress as though the gun had left behind some type of residue she wanted no part of.

"Listen Carlos, I um," she studied the gun for a second more and then shook her head and rounded on him. "I really appreciate the offer to get away but I can't right now- not with all the stuff I've got on my plate-" what remained of her spiel was interrupted by a shriek when his hands closed on her arms and squeezed.

"All I expect you to do," he began in the cool, succinct manner that few had ever dared argue with, "is check your bags-be sure I didn't forget to pack anything you really need, meet me downstairs and forget Ty's trip and Josephine's wedding," he gave her a quick once-over. "I have serious doubts you'll be able to attend it much less organize it."

Fueled by a few lingering remnants of her earlier courage, Dena wrenched free of his loosening hold. "I guess I should apologize for giving you cause to think being my husband gives you the right to rule me, but I'm done with that Carlos. I've already let you keep me from my family enough. I'm done."

Carlos studied the beauty before him with an evolved appreciation. "I'm glad to hear you say that, D." His rakish smile deepened at the surprise he saw registering on her face. "I'll take it to mean that you're... done with keeping all those parts of your life hidden from me. Looks like you're finally strong enough to come clean. Change your clothes, check your bags, meet me downstairs," he moved closer while running down the order. "We've got a long drive. Maybe along the way, you can tell me who put their hands on you and left proof behind. Take a look in the mirror, babe." He brushed a thumb along the wicked bruise across her cheek and then turned his back on her.

"You got twenty minutes," he called over his shoulder and stopped off to collect his gun from the endtable. "Thanks for the reassemble," he said on his way out the bedroom door.

***

Dena wasted ten of the twenty minutes Carlos gave her for last minute packing. She stood in the mirror following his cryptic comment about someone touching her and leaving behind proof.

Eva was right, she thought brushing the back of her hand across the pronounced darkening of skin below her eye.

"Damn you, Maeva," she smirked, acknowledging how meaningless the words were.

She had a much bigger problem then. Such as, what she was going to tell Carlos about that bruise. The question gave her a moment of pause and she thought of her husband then. More specifically, she thought of the look in his nearly translucent eyes when he mentioned the bruise and touched her besides. He'd been calm. Not that she would have preferred him beating his chest and storming out for vengeance, only there was something… off about his behavior.

"Ten minutes, D!"

His voice thundering up, launched Dena into movement and she was then in search of her phone. It didn't take long for her to realize that not only was her mobile missing but a quick check of the phone connected to the land line produced no dial tone.

"Son of a-" Closing her eyes, Dena dragged her thumbnail across her brow and prayed for calm. She was still holding the cordless when Carlos returned to the bedroom.

"What the hell are you up to?" She shook the phone for emphasis. "Where are we going?"

"Away."

Carlos apparently possessed droves of the calm Dena was trying to summon for herself. "What's going on with you?" Expression curious, she shook her head in wonder. "Why aren't you pissed about my face?"

"Oh I'm pissed, D," like a switch flipping, his demeanor changed. Dena dropped the phone, backing toward the wall when he advanced.

"I'm goddamned pissed as fuck and the last thing I need while trying to get the truth out of you is one of your never ending stream of family dropping by, calling, texting or parachuting in for a chat." He had her snug between the wall and the imposing breadth of his frame then.

"I can promise you babe, you're about to find out just how pissed I am, but this isn't the place I want to share that with you. Get your shit and let's go." With unnatural grace, he backed away, turned and snagged the cases near the door. He draped the straps of all five bags across his shoulders and left the room.

Dena maintained her post near the wall, eyes wide, expression worried.

***

Outside Mt. Hood, Oregon~

"Oregon? We're going to Oregon?" Dena was incredulous and could no longer stifle the urge to comment. Besides, she'd managed for long enough.

It seemed they had been driving for hours. Despite her earlier boldness, she hadn't dared to ask Carlos a thing- including whether or not he'd scheduled bathroom breaks for their little road trip. He hadn't spoken a word since they'd walked out of the front door. Once they hit the Interstate that Carlos had selected to carry them off to parts unknown, he'd even shut down the Suburban's radio. The smooth drone of the vehicle's engine was more jarring than relaxing yet clearly Carlos was in no mood for chatter. Well... none that touched on any subject Dena was aching to discuss with him. Coolly, she ruffled her hair in an effort to masquerade grazing her fingers across her bruised cheek.

No, she wasn't aching to approach the subject he preferred, at all. Regardless, she would have to come up with something to tell him and obviously he wasn't going to buy that she'd accidentally run into a wall. A voice feathered in to propose she tell him the truth, the suggestion encouraged her to fidget against the cab's suede seating.

It was time to be forthright- she recognized that. It was *past* time. If she couldn't trust the man she'd loved all her life with the deepest and darkest, then who *could* she trust? Besides, Evangela was right, her family was a team of investigators and damn good ones if all they'd uncovered over the past few years was any proof.

Too much was hitting too close to home- a home in which she'd stored a throng of ugly memorabilia from her past. What would they think of her? What would Carlos think? Would he understand that she owed them? Would he understand that some debts had to be paid whether by those who had incurred them or by the ones they left behind?

~CHAPTER FOUR~

Mt. Hood, Oregon~

Although autumn's nip had already made its grand
entrance in Seattle, things were still relatively mild. Little
more than a jacket was needed in the early morning or
evening hours. An icy wind and light dusting of snow
proved that Mt. Hood had fully opened its doors to winter.

Dena knew that her husband's work and his
proficiency at it had amassed him a small fortune over the
years. Aware of his love for camping and the outdoors, she
hadn't been surprised that he'd had a propensity for
acquiring properties in wooded areas.

The cabin he kept in Nova Scotia for instance, had
been a welcomed surprise. It was a much needed oasis
following his reappearance in her life after the fiasco
involving her sister-in-law Nile and the men who had
promised death to them both unless Nile produced a set of

card keys linking various prominent figures to an under aged brothel Nile's father ran in Nice, France.

Carlos' quick thinking and killing skill had saved their lives. That night, marked a new beginning for their shattered relationship. Carlos had taken her to the cabin in Nova Scotia where they spent two weeks before he'd whisked her away to another of his outdoorsy acquisitions. Dena recalled that romantic escape with a smile. It had lasted almost two months and then they were off again- their destination toward tropical waters where they took long overdue vows and Dena happily changed her last name from Ramsey to McPhereson. Yet, for all their jet-setting, they had not visited the property in the line of Dena's sight just then.

"It's not mine," Carlos silenced the GMCs engine while answering her unspoken question. "It was used for something else once," he didn't bother to throw on a jacket over the black flannel shirt he wore with gray Carpenter's jeans. He left Dena to ponder the remark and went to take their bags from the rear of the SUV.

The metallic clang of the rear doors being unhinged, galvanized Dena into action and she opened the passenger door. The sound of her boots crushing the smattering of snow underfoot seemed to echo across the terrain. A terrain Dena observed as being almost completely wooded.

How the devil did he find his way out here? She hadn't seen him using any sort of GPS. There wasn't any real path- no evident road or even a gravel trail marked by grooves worn in by repetitive tire tracks.

What is this place? She wasn't sure she really wanted an answer to her silent question. The place was the perfect setting for a gruesome horror movie that was for sure, she thought.

"This is the *last* place I'd want to have a break down," she muttered, eyeing the environment with increasing wariness.

"That's the idea," Carlos had secured the tailgate and was joining Dena at the vehicle's passenger side.

"Are you sure about leaving the car here?" *Or us for that matter?* She pushed suddenly chilled hands into the deep pockets of her ankle length sweater coat, covering the jeans and turtleneck she wore.

Carlos was already heading toward the imposing dwelling. "I'll come back before dark and put it in the garage," without shifting his gaze from his intended destination, he pointed east toward another structure.

Dena followed his gesture and saw a shed that appeared to be holding landscaping equipment. Dena figured it'd be pointless to ask whether the stuff had gotten any use. There was an abundance of space for at least two vehicles to be stored.

"Hope the place has great security. We're gonna need it out here," she gave another uncertain observation of their surroundings.

"The place is as hard to get into as it is to get out of."

His helpful acknowledgement wasn't reassuring. "That's what I was afraid of," Dena sighed, resolvedly following Carlos up the steep porch steps.

He didn't produce a key and she saw that there was no need. The door appeared to have no knobs or levers of any kind. Moreover, it appeared to be made of some type of reinforced steel. Iron, perhaps? The entire surface was finished in a brownish shellacked substance that; from a distance, gave it an inviting wooden appearance.

Dena recognized docile beeps coming from the door. Carlos was entering a code to a keypad on a small black box that flashed vivid green numbers. The box was affixed mid-way down the far right of the door the way a knob would be. The code was accepted and the heavy door slid open without a sound. Carlos gave a makeshift wave-urging Dena to precede him.

"Carlos-"

"Inside."

She obliged.

***

"I was thinking you might…get together and discuss the case or… I don't know- something following all the fireworks in Scotland." Roman Tesano checked the soufflé he had been attempting for a late supper with his wife Imani. He spoke in the direction of a sleek black speaker that appeared to be built into a side panel along the cooking island where he toiled.

"You could've even extended the trip," Roman continued, "Scotland's a beautiful place, especially in winter."

In Brooklyn, New York Caiphus Tesano chuckled over his father's words. He set the cordless; he'd been carrying through his uncle's apartment, to rest in the crook of his neck. "You've been reading too many of Mommy's romance novels." He grinned.

"Do you still love her?"

"Yes," Caiphus answered his father's question without hesitation or regret.

Roman laughed. "Then it's not as far off from *Mommy's romances* as you might think. Tell Pitch we'll talk later. I love you."

"Love you too," Caiphus regarded the phone for a second or two once the connection ended.

"Smoak says your brain goes numb when you've got her on it."

Caiphus' grin refreshed at the sound of his uncle's voice. He tossed the phone to the sofa where he had taken up space since paying a visit to Pitch Tesano. His thoughts turned to his older brother then and he shook his head.

"That's just Smoak's way of saying I'm an idiot because she's *always* on my mind."

Pitch passed his youngest nephew a bottle of Red Oak. He tilted his own back to down a healthy swig while settling his towering frame into his preferred armchair.

"Well maybe when this is over-"

"No Unk," Caiphus was already shaking his head. "It'll never be over, not for her and because of that, not for me either."

Pitch smoothed a hand down the seam of the worn gray sweats he sported around the house and shifted into a more comfortable position on the chair. "Why'd you come see me tonight?"

"There was an old case," Caiphus balanced his beer bottle on a jean clad knee. "It surfaced back when I was getting my feet wet with Dad's shop."

"*Your* shop," Pitch corrected as a reminder to Caiphus that; even surrounded by family, he was encouraged to remember that *he* was the man who ran the show.

"My shop," Caiphus tilted the bottle in toast. "But back when Dad was involved," he waited for Pitch's approving nod.

"I had more time to devote to a case that merged in with something Bee; and her team were at work on, and just like that," the snap of his fingers echoed in the room, "all our leads dried up, vanished or died- literally."

Intrigue froze Pitch's chiseled dark copper-toned face over the span of several seconds. When a question seemed imminent, Caiphus presented the folder he'd brought along when he'd arrived at the condo.

"This is all way too freaky and weird to try verbally explaining. You may absorb it better by reading." The smile Caiphus mustered was grim at best.

Pitch set aside his beer, exchanging it for the thick folder secured by an extra-large binder clip. He whistled when he hefted the collection of documents. "How long have you been at work on this, kid?"

"Before or *after* I was encouraged to stop?"

"And you say SyBilla is involved?" Pitch was unclipping the folder.

"Her team made a drug bust that uncovered things that gave our cases a common element. But she was a part of it before then."

Pitch left the folder alone and waited.

"That old case uncovered a lead to Black Island by way of a ship owned by Cufi Muhammad... and Marc Ramsey."

"Fuck," Pitch settled back against the recliner with such force, the chair creaked.

"By the time we put everything together," Caiphus went on, "the bastard had already transferred his ownership of the damn thing to his son Fernando." He shrugged. "We didn't want to link Fern to that so we didn't act on it and then there was Bee and-"

"She's a Ramsey too and that just makes it all kinds of complicated," Pitch finished.

Caiphus nodded. "And that's especially true when she's doing her own sideline digging that's bringing her closer to my investigations."

For a while there was only the sound of Pitch's heel clapping the sole of his flip flops. "What does she know?"

"That Vale is a part of it and at a time when all we'd been able to uncover were the scraps of small-time muscle Gabe was letting him flex or so we thought. The fact that we let him slide with that and then he turns up

56

with a connection to the island… it's part of the reason she doesn't trust me to this day."

"And was she *encouraged* to leave the case alone as well?"

Caiphus' sapphire gaze flashed with old regret and he mopped a hand over his face. "Lamont made a show of ordering us all to shut it down."

"And was that on your order?" Pitch's mouth crooked into a knowing smile.

Caiphus waved a hand defiantly. "I swear it was fully Lamont's call. But I agreed- you bet your ass I agreed." Clenching a fist, he worked it into his palm.

"A man was killed- shortly after leaving our tanks at Vestige. We'd detained him in connection to the case," Caiphus rested his head back on the sofa and studied the recessed lighting dotting the ceiling of the living room. "He was shot to death in his car… after that we just wanted to regroup and there were-" He blinked and gave a fast shake of his head. "We had other issues to handle."

Pitch bowed his head, understanding that the 'other issues' his nephew mentioned had nothing to do with the oversight committee his brother Roman had devised to investigate the more suspect dealings of the Tesano family. Pitch remembered the challenges faced by his brother's family as a result of the accident suffered by Roman's wife Imani. It had been discovered that the accident which; until recently had left Imani wheelchair bound, had been the fault of Pitch's other nephew Brogue Tesano.

There were however, other issues relating to Roman's eldest son Hilliam. Pitch sensed that subject was what Caiphus had really come to discuss.

"He won't come back to us," Caiphus must have sensed his uncle tapping into his train of thought. "Not until he destroys it."

"The tentacles of this monster are far-reaching and they've had grips on our boy more times than even *he* probably realizes." Pitch shifted his dark and bottomless eyes toward the case folder.

"Through a combination of luck and skill, Hill has managed to detach himself and hasn't gotten himself swallowed up in all that foolishness- maybe it's in his best interest to remain detached."

Caiphus blurted an ill-humored laugh. "Come on, Unk. You know he won't do that. Especially when he thinks destroying the family corruption is the only way to atone for Persephone and Mommy."

"Strong men and their weaknesses," Pitch lamented. "Hmph... Achilles had one, so did Sampson- we won't get started on mine," his smile was sad, haunted.

"Your mother and Persephone are Hill's." Pitch finished his beer, fixing Caiphus with a steady look the entire time. "I know you see him, Cai and that he confides in you."

Caiphus sat up a bit straighter on the sofa.

Pitch dipped his head, accepting Caiphus' reaction as confirmation of his suspicions. "In that case, it'd be wise of you to remind your brother that going after the family in that cock-sure, ballsy way of his would surely put Imani and Persephone in harm's way- in *Vale's* way. My little brother may be a self-absorbed son of a bitch, but Hump put him in charge because his love of depravity is legend. He runs a tight ship and few have the nerve to cross him. This needs to be done with as much brawn as it does finesse- that's where *you* come in and Hill needs to understand that. It's going to be hard enough finding even one person to guide you toward which wires to cut."

"Right," Caiphus rubbed a hand through the dark cottony forest of his hair. "I guess I should get started on trying to find that *one* then."

***

The cabin's uninviting exterior in no way carried over to its interior design. Glistening dark hardwoods were accentuated by expansive and intricately fashioned throw rugs. The rustic appeal of the place was further perpetuated by the richly, paneled walls. The furnishings were a mix of posh suede and comfy tweed. Most of the seating was extra-long and reinforced by sturdy pine siding. It had obviously been built to suit extremely tall and heavy bodies.

Dena risked a glance at her husband, instantly riveted on the fluid grace with which he moved. He had an extraordinary manner for someone so large. She realized the asset was one of the many things that made him so lethal.

"Sure is cozy in here," she returned to observing the place when he glanced her way. "You wouldn't expect this from the outside." She slipped out of the sweater coat and draped it over the back of a chair.

Carlos was squatted before the substantial hearth in a far corner of the room. Dena watched him reaching up into the fireplace apparently searching for the flue.

"It's important to first set a tone of calm," he shared, locating the flue and disengaging the hatch.

"Are you um," she swallowed, watching as he used an ornately carved poker to dig around in the soot and ash left behind from a previous blaze. "Are you referring to the calm before a storm?" She tentatively ventured toward an explanation for what was to be expected.

She'd taken a seat on the arm of one of the wide armchairs situated closest to the fireplace. The vantage point allowed her to see the lopsided grin re-defining the already sultry curve of his mouth.

"That would depend," he at last responded to her question.

"On what?"

"On how long it takes for you to share what you're keeping from me?"

"Carlos-"

"It's why we're here. You know that."

"But why here?" She scooted forward a little on the chair's arm. "Why this place? Whatever you think I'm keeping could've been discussed at home."

"Could it?" He turned a bit, but didn't leave his spot before the fireplace. "You haven't taken advantage of that convenience yet and since I'm tired of waiting, more radical action seemed to be a good idea."

"How radical?" Her dark eyes narrowed in observance of the room's high ceilings. "What is this place? What are we gonna do here and *please*," she extended a hand, "don't tell me that all depends on me."

There was quiet for a time as Carlos prepared to start the fire. He one-handed enormous logs across a vast grate and then rose to take one of the long matches from a tall wrought iron cylinder that perched on the wide stone mantle.

Dena shivered, not yet feeling the surge of warmth sure to stir from the massive flames that were beginning to pop and lick the blackened sides of the hearth.

Carlos dropped the used match into the fire and then rounded on her. "We're going to do all kinds of things here," his beckoning pale greens were fixed, locking her into an inescapable bond. "How much you enjoy them will depend on how much you tell me."

In spite of her unease, Dena couldn't ignore the sensation beginning to hum at the heart of her. "I didn't know games like that did anything for you."

He shrugged, the move barely sending a ripple through the fabric of his shirt. "Guess that goes to show there's a lot we don't know about each other. But you can be sure my techniques get amazing results," his voice softened as he leaned against the mantelpiece.

"Is that what you use this place for?" She stiffened, drawing on whatever anger she could muster. "Getting results and *benefitting* from your technique?"

He moved, dwarfing her where she still perched on the armchair. "This place is for those unfortunates who think I'm just kidding around when I politely ask to be told the truth."

Dena kept her expression schooled but inside the humming sensations at her core thrummed with a vibrant beat. She didn't believe a woman alive would deem it 'unfortunate' to be brought there for the precise purpose of having Carlos McPhereson use his…techniques to get the truth out of her.

Somewhere amidst the humming however, uncertainty began its subtle surge. The cozy dwelling gradually betrayed signs of that lingering uninviting cloud around its edges.

"I'd like to see if you're wearing any other bruises besides the ones on your face." His voice was still maddeningly soft but unnerving nonetheless.

The request had a jarring effect. "Carlos-"

"Shh…enough talk for one day," he was already focused on the buttons adorning the bodice of the mauve capped-sleeve sweater she wore.

It occurred to her then how long the day had actually been. The realization was exhausting and her breath raced as if she were all of a sudden laboring to catch it. Her lashes felt heavy yet she fought against letting them shield her gaze. Carlos was inside her sweater then. His fingers were getting lost in the valley between her breasts that heaved as she worked to steady her breathing.

Working to steady her breathing was a pointless feat given the fact that he was touching her. His touch merely

61

intensified what she hoped to quell. Her lashes were set on a constant flutter, replicating the beat of her heart just then. Her body tensed, arching into a bow, anticipating a more thorough exploration.

"Stand up," he tugged her from the arm of the chair before she could comply.

"Take this off," he pulled the sweater's hem.

Dena relaxed in response to the instruction, reverting into playful mode while closing the remaining distance between them. "Why don't you do it?" She nudged his chest with hers.

Carlos moved back a step and simply watched her, his gaze coolly expectant as he waited. She cooperated, regressing into the uncertainty that had claimed her for most of the day.

"Everything," he clarified once Dena had finished with the sweater and stood twisting the garment in her hand. She'd pulled the sweater over her head which sent healthy lush tresses tumbling about her exquisite face. In that instant, his every intention was re-directed on the desire she could so smoothly instill. Wearing a grimace, he freed the sweater sending it to the hardwoods visible just beyond a corner of a broad rug.

Claiming her upper arm, Carlos drew her away from the chair, giving himself room to walk a circle around Dena as she doffed what remained of her clothes.

She accomplished the task much sooner than she'd expected what with her hands trembling as terribly as they'd been. She understood then why he hadn't remained in the bedroom while she changed clothes earlier. He'd had something more in mind. The inviting warmth from the fire that battled the heavy chill of the cabin did nothing to cease the shivers riddling through her.

Carlos traced the tip of a middle finger along the graceful dip of Dena's spine and allowed the touch to laze about the small of her back for a short while. Dena watched as he; unmindful of the clothing pooled at her feet, moved in. Thoroughly, he crushed her finely made garb beneath a large hiking boot. His hand at her spine, curved around gliding over her hip to hook her upper thigh.

"Carlos..." she practically whimpered his name, aching to turn.

"Quiet," his hand flexed at her thigh, briefly tightening almost to the point of discomfort.

Her head felt heavy and Dena prayed he wouldn't begrudge her resting back against the reassuring breadth of his chest. Her sharp inhale colored the room when his thumb launched a beautiful assault on her labia. The silky, licorice folds soon held a slight sheen of liquid arousal as a result of his attention.

As the affecting thumb attentively carried out its actions, Carlos lent his middle finger to the task, barely dipping it in to test the building moisture that laced the tip of his finger. He spread her dewy response across her thigh upon withdrawing.

Dena had been clenching fists at her sides. She then reached back to gather handfuls of his loose fitting jeans as she bucked lightly in an attempt to steal more pleasure from his touch.

Unable to adequately resist her and in no way surprised by the fact, Carlos gave in to her unspoken request. His hold remained firm at her thigh when he feathered kisses down her neck and across the feminine slope of her shoulders. Boldly, a thick middle finger returned for an encore and he presented the repeat performance with a possessive fervor.

"Yes...mmm...Los..." Her shuddery groans carried over the snap of the logs ablaze in the hearth. She worked her body up and down the lone seducing finger without an ounce of shame. Her lips parted to twin provocative bows, emitting trace moans and weak gasps.

Dena bit her lip then on the sudden tensing that preface orgasm. Her heart raced in anticipation of the shattering explosion that...never arrived.

"Carlos?" His name on her tongue held unmistakable disbelief when he denied her his touch thus depriving her of what had the makings of a delectable climax. The fact that he would deny her that sweet concession was beyond unexpected. Agitated by unsatisfied need, Dena had little time to ponder his motives before she felt him scooping her up only to drop her without second thought to one of the tweed sofas the room claimed.

Her next sharp intake of breath had nothing to do with arousal or disappointment and everything to do with devastation. Carlos was hunched above her yet made no move to touch. Instead, expectancy once again pooled his exquisite eyes. He appeared to be measuring her reaction to the sudden turn of events and more.

Blinking incessantly, her hair splayed the sofa cushions as she worked to make sense of the images flashing inside her head. "Your gun..." she breathed the words as though the two phrases alone were enough to draw the answer she sought from him.

Apparently she was right.

"You took it." He said.

More blinking and then she stilled, her eyes widening. The expressive onyx orbs were riveted upon his face, working over every powerfully chiseled inch until additional discovery settled.

"I took it," her tone was affirming.

"Tell me how," he encouraged but took no offense when she looked away in clear denial of his request. He smiled as if her reaction was one he'd expected.

Dena was far too stunned by the more violent events that had occurred between her and her husband earlier that day. Until that moment, they had been forgotten. Yes, she thought the truth was definitely the only thing he would accept.

Evidently, Carlos was in no hurry to receive his truths just then. The tug of his skillful mouth at her nipples threw Dena's senses into overdrive right alongside those of shock and nervousness currently at work within her. His big hands loosely cupped her breasts as he suckled hungrily. The long sleek line of his brows drew close to emphasize his utter focus on the enjoyable task before him. His thumb worked the nipple he'd yet to tend to keeping it firm and ready for when its turn at pleasure arrived.

Dena wanted to absorb every thrilling ounce of enjoyment his lips and tongue stirred. The intense wet feasting at her chest had her suffering the effects of labored breathing once again. She wanted to feel the awesome form of his body against hers and began to elicit light tugs on his shirt.

Carlos stifled his wife's hopes then. His voice rained down like an icy blast of water to sun-drenched skin. "You'll tell me," he spoke into her skin. "You'll tell me all of it D. Finding out what I want to know is what I do best." He resumed the affecting suckle at her glistening nipples for another excruciatingly pleasurable moment.

"Don't worry," he said when she was all but sobbing for him to give her release. "I think you'll enjoy my methods as much as I will."

~CHAPTER FIVE~

"You're not serious?"

Their budding encounter on the living room sofa had ended abruptly, but Dena still held onto the hope of things resuming their course when Carlos carried her upstairs. Her amazed question was all she'd been able to utter when he deposited her naked on top of a broad sleigh bed, tossed over a black fleece blanket and headed for the room's double doors once he'd bid her goodnight.

"Carlos?!" Her voice had raised a clear octave, disbelief rendering her virtually immovable atop the bed's wine colored comforter.

"You're coming back." Her tone was all knowing.

Halting in the doorway, he reclined against the frame. "You need your rest."

"Where are *you* going to sleep?"

"My room's just down the hall."

Her jaw dropped, the confirmation stirring a virtually non-existent temper. "You want your answers so badly that you can't even sleep with me?"

"I want my answers so badly that I don't *trust* myself to sleep with you." To himself, Carlos confessed that he would surely lose his mind and focus being inside her. He stood there watching her naked atop that bed, looking like a confection he wanted to devour and knew he'd want to be no place else, thinking of nothing else but her.

"So that's your plan?" Her abrupt laughter held no humor. "Deny us both until I crack under pressure and give you this truth you're seeking?"

"Is the truth so upsetting that you'd have to crack before sharing it?" His tone was soft, solemn.

Dena held her head in her hands as though she were completely exasperated. Expelling a loud breath, she tossed her hair out of her face and let him see the stoniness filtering her eyes. "Just remember that I'm your wife and not one of the bail jumping idiots you and Moses chase half way around the world."

His easy stance went rigid and in the next moment he was closing the distance to the bed. There, he hunched over Dena again, sending her back against the headboard. "The reason I ever even considered chasing bail jumping idiots was because it kept me close to you in my own idiotic way," his voice was gravel.

"But you can believe it wasn't out of an overwhelming love for your family. I go way back with Moses but what I've done for him and anyone else who's required my help gave me a way to keep tabs on you."

He bowed his head just a fraction and Dena was fixed on the jagged dance of the muscle along his square jaw.

"I hoped all that would bring you back to me and it has," he moved closer wanting her to see the thinly veiled wave of upset behind his eyes. "All the shit I've done has damn well earned me the truth. It'd be smart for you to think about how much longer you want to keep it from me. I'm a patient man, D but as you've pointed out, you're my wife and as I now have a vested interest in the truth, my methods may become a little more creative."

She eased the blanket in place across her breasts when his stare rested there for an extended period. "I'm not afraid of you," she said.

"I know babe," his smile was genuine and adoring and he helped her tuck the blanket in around her breasts. "It would kill me if you were, but you don't trust me-"

"I-"

"You're afraid you'll lose me if you spill it all. You're so wrapped up in that belief that it's burying you. I'll use any means to break through that." The softness in his smile hardened with what took control of his expression then.

"I'll use anything to weaken what's tying down your emotion. All I need is to find that loose thread and tug it."

"And you'd use how much we want to-to be together to do that?" She searched his face for her answer. He moved in to nibble at her earlobe then and she melted into the array of pillows at her back.

"The tug will be just enough...just enough to have you begging me to free the tie," his nose trailed the line of her neck, "but that'll only happen when you trust me."

Tears caused her eyes to sparkle like glinting pools of onyx. "I do trust you," she clutched his shirt for emphasis.

Carlos kissed the spot beneath her ear. "Not enough. Get some sleep," he shut off the lighting and left her alone in the dark.

It was a long while before sleep visited Dena.

***

Quinto do Lago, Portugal~

"This could backfire on us, you know?" Saffron Manoa waited for the explosion sure to follow for merely insinuating that her boss' plan had a few weak spots.

Surprisingly, Evangela showed no signs of exploding when she took a seat on one of the rockers dotting the front porch that extended along the sides and rear of the villa.

"I think Dena's too afraid of losing that piece of eye candy she calls a husband." She shared following a few moments of idle rocking.

"But we all know he's more than that," Although pleased to be taken into the woman's confidence as opposed to being snarled at over voicing a reasonable point, Saffron still treaded carefully. "He isn't a man we'd want for an enemy."

"We need to get to Perjas," Evangela leaned forward in the rocker, dragging her fingers through her hair while resting her elbows against the satiny lounge pants she sported. "Time's getting short."

"For who?" Saffron still treaded with care. "There's a lot at stake, you know?"

"I do," Evangela's voice harbored an unusual weariness. "And I know something has to be done about Mae."

"Do you think whatever's out there will help her?"

Evangela didn't answer.

"Do you think Dena will be motivated to help based on the fact that there's more of the drug that helped her with those headaches and dreams?" Saffron tried.

"Saf," Eva's smile held sudden cunning and she reached over to tug on one of Saffron's reddish brown dreadlocks. "You know as well as I do that the drug was what caused the headaches in the first place. I only mentioned it to get a reaction from her," she began rocking the chair again.

"She's been off it a long time. She's doing fine- I could see it in her eyes. What's happening to Mae was set in motion long ago..." Evangela shook off whatever else had crossed her mind then.

"Those dreams of Denny's," she went on, "well they were just a side effect of an ugly moment in the life of a little princess."

"A little princess who has a lot of power behind her. They're really close to... closing in on it all."

Evangela waved off Saffron's concerns. "They don't know the half of it. They're hell set on destroying the island in the most humane way possible since to completely obliterate it means putting lots of innocent lives in jeopardy. The kids still there aren't at fault just part of a larger picture." She left the rocker to occupy a spot along the porch railing.

"That place has to be destroyed from the top down and by taking out the vermin who created it." She drew on another heap of cunning when she smiled. "First thing Dena and her powerhouse will need to know is who all the players are and then they'll need to *discuss* how best to take 'em down and then they'll need to put the plan into action. All that *plotting* just buys us time."

Saffron grinned. "So essentially we're using them to farm out the job of taking down the vermin for us?"

"Why not?" Evangela shrugged. "We'll have our hands full enough trying to locate this research camp."

"But you don't think it's on the island someplace?" Saffron smiled at the look her boss shifted her way.

"Hell no," Evangela winked. "Why do you think I told Denny about it? They'll go after the island first anyway just to be diligent in the hopes of finding something that might lead them to whatever the hell they think I'm on to."

"But won't Captain Perjas talk to them about it?"

"Not all of it," Evangela studied the expanse of palm trees dotting the front yard. "He was long gone by the time it was established- his work was the foundation for it, though but he went to continue his research elsewhere. He knows though...he damn well knows the research and I need to know if it does what I think it does before I risk putting our asses in the wind for it. I need him to tell me about his researchers- the ones who used Re-Gen in their own studies. It's like they just-just vanished." She gave an agitated shake of her head. "How is that possible, Saf? There's no one we can't find."

"Perjas managed to evade us, you know?" Saffron reminded her.

"Right..." Evangela smoothed her hand across her cheek. "And that's why we're gonna have a chat with him about where they are."

She returned to the rocker. "We've made a good life for ourselves because we're a group of smart bitches. That fuck up with Lee and Rafe in Scotland proves we need smarter folks to handle our tasks."

"Genius assassins, who'd have thunk it," Saffron teased, then gradually sobered. "So we're letting him off the hook about the rest? Who all's involved, where they are? How do you even *know* Perjas a.k.a. Stone still isn't part of the whole mess?"

"Because it went against why he started the island in the first place."

Saffron's warm gaze narrowed in wonder. "How do you know all this?"

"Oh Saf," Evangela hugged herself. "I've always been a fan of information. You just never know when it'll come in handy."

"Or who might come after you for knowing it," Saffron cautioned.

Just then, Lula Velez and Santi Dumont arrived on the porch. Lula sported an arm in a sling while Santi hobbled on a crutch to support the cast boot on her left leg.

"You're right," Evangela slanted another wink in Saffron's direction and then looked to her other associates. "How are you guys doin'?"

"We're livin'," Lula said while Santi hobbled to one of the rockers lining the porch.

"Any word on Casper?" Evangela asked Saffron.

"I've been monitoring the databases of all the hospitals within a fifty mile radius of the DeBurgh property." Saffron sighed, folding her legs beneath her on the rocker she occupied. "I even broadened the scope to include the whole of Scotland and nothing. Only Rain has been accounted for."

Silence held for a time as the women remembered their fallen associate.

"Stay on it," Evangela ordered, pointing a manicured index finger toward Saffron. "You're right. We *don't* know who might come after us for what we know." She looked to Santi and Lula.

"How soon before you two are up to another job?"

The women traded looks. "Very soon," Santi replied.

"Good," Evangela gave a curt nod. "Because this is something we can't farm out. It may be time to tie up loose ends- *all* loose ends. If anybody gets caught dangling it sure as hell won't be one of us."

***

"Is she okay?" The smooth depth of Taurus Ramsey's voice held equal portions of concern and ferocity when he inquired of his sister.

"She's good," Carlos spoke to his brother-in-law through the other end of an untraceable landline, "we just needed to get away- some things we needed to talk about."

"Are you guys alright?" Taurus' concern overcame more of the fierceness coloring his voice.

"Fine," Carlos understood that Taurus was referring to the state of their marriage. "It's not easy to get a woman to share her secrets, you know?"

"Ha! Don't I," From his end of the line, Taurus recalled that it was next to impossible as memories surfaced of the obstacles he and Nile had to face. Taurus knew that his sister and her husband had been battling such obstacles since they were kids. He could only imagine the enormity of secrets that must reside between them.

"Would you give Josephine a call?" Carlos asked his brother-in-law. "D's handling her wedding stuff-"

"Don't sweat it. We'll work it out, but we're gonna miss having you guys here-trip won't be the same without you," Taurus said, referring to the impromptu pre-holiday couple's getaway they'd been treated to courtesy of Tykira Ramsey's clients. "Sabra's very... concerned." He joined in when his brother-in-law began to chuckle at his cousin's expense. "So do I need to tell Moses anything?"

"Nah, thanks T I'll um-I'll handle it. I don't want anybody worried so let's keep this as quiet as we can, alright?"

"Understood. Take care of our girl."

"I promise," Carlos grinned. "Thanks, man." Once disconnected, Carlos returned the receiver to the CB apparatus nestled along a cubby in a darkened corridor beneath the basement stairwell. He would give Moses a call soon and that would have to suffice for all the contact he'd intended with the outside world. This part of the cabin was the very last place he wanted to spend an abundance of time.

And what about spilling all your secrets? The toneless question caused him to bristle. His wife knew he'd *done* things-loathsome things. She hadn't judged or fallen out of love with him because of them. He'd known she wouldn't. Of course, it was one thing to know *of* evil deeds and another thing entirely to have all the dirty details of how they were carried out.

Being in this place, he studied the patches of mildew caked between the wooden planks and bricks and thought of the horrors those walls would share if they could. They were horrors he'd often choreographed in pursuit of hidden truths for the purpose of justice. Justice and answers, he thought bringing Dena back into the forefront of his mind.

The diligence he'd given to his... profession had rewarded him with a highly regarded name in certain circles. Carlos had never given a damn about reputation. It had all been for her, to find her, what took her from him? Why? And who, besides her corrupt father and uncle were responsible?

Until then, he had never come so close to discovering the last but he needed her to come clean. That was the true challenge in all this. Given what he *did* know, Dena would never volunteer information no matter how 'creative' his methods became. She was too afraid she'd lose him, lose what neither of them ever thought they'd recapture.

She knew there was nothing she could tell him that would make him let her go. She knew that, but she didn't trust it. As waiting patiently hadn't done the trick, a larger jolt was required. He'd played the game before. Everyone had a breaking point. True, women oftentimes required a little more creative coaxing, but the desired results often followed.

This though, was a game he had never played with his wife- a woman he'd been addicted to since forever. Withholding had not been easy-almost a week had passed and he was practically out of his mind needing her. He could only hope she would give in before he did.

~~~

Dena thought the bed slept wonderfully, but would have slept far better had Carlos been sharing it with her. She had to give credit to his plan- using what they'd found between each other. Denying sex to… encourage her to share the simple truth. But the truth was rarely that simple. If it were, everyone would practice it and there would be a world of saints.

She smiled, shifting her position beneath the sheets and taking yet another survey of the room that was to be hers for who knew how long. They wouldn't be disturbed out there, that was for sure. Just as sure, was the fact that he'd leave her once she told him everything he *thought* he wanted to hear.

The stained wooden door opened with a creak. Dena stayed where she was in bed, intentionally keeping her back to the door.

"Ready for breakfast?" He asked from where he stood just inside the room.

"Ready to go home," she murmured.

Carlos crossed to the bed, trailed fingers across her shoulder drawing down the sheet as he went. "Are you ready to talk to me?"

With a sigh, Dena turned over bracing her weight on her elbow and glaring up at him. "I have the strangest feeling that you already know what I'm going to say. There're parts of what happened between us at the house that had already slipped my mind and I'm guessing you had that missing info the whole time."

He joined her on the bed then, working the muscle beneath his jaw and trying desperately to keep his eyes away from her exposed chest. "Your florist told me there were two women on their way out when she was just getting there. I go in and find the den a mess and then you attacked me."

"God..." her heartbeat raged in her ears.

"This is where you reciprocate, Dena."

Her eyes fixed on the faded pro football emblem on the T-shirt he wore. "It was Eva Leer and her sidekick Mae. They were behind what happened in Scotland and in Vegas with Smoak and Sabra."

"I know this, D."

She laughed. "'Course you do!"

"Why'd they come to see you?"

Averting her stare, Dena tried to shift her position between the covers again. He took her arm, squeezing a bit while giving her the slightest shake. "In Scotland, they would've taken Contessa and Darby, used them to hurt Fern and Kraven. Why would they come to the house just for a chat and not take you?"

She gave a flirty toss of her hair. "I'm not on their hit list, I guess."

"So? What'd they want?" He persisted, watching her bristle as she braced against his hold on her arm. "We don't leave until I get what I want."

"And what about what *I* want?" She whined, trailing her eyes across the chords of muscle lining his thick arms and feeling her arousal course from the sight. His

resulting smile filled her with dismay instead of elation.
She knew he had no intentions of following through on
whatever manner of teasing he'd planned to subject her to
that day.

Still, she welcomed the sensual path his nose began
to trek across her collarbone. All the while, his hand moved
to smother a breast and commence a sultry molestation of
her nipple beneath his thumb.

"Carlos," she whispered. "Don't, plea-" her mouth
was filled with his tongue, verbal communication halted for
the moment.

Eagerly, she moved to link her arms about his neck,
paying no mind to the sheet drifting down to pool at her
waist. Never breaking the kiss, Carlos tugged her arms
from his neck and then eased her down into the abundant
pillows and crisp linens. His skillful mouth blazed an erotic
journey across her collarbone and then down into the deep
valley between the rapid rise and fall of her breasts.

He let go of her arms and Dena eased them beneath
the cool pillows as she luxuriated in his touch. Her hips
performed a wicked dance beneath the covers and she
arched sharply when his lips covered the nipple his thumb
had just assaulted.

"Carlos..."

"Talk to me, D," he spoke around the nipple that
glistened and puckered for him. "Talk to me and I'll take
you home..."

She moved her head against the pillows in
resistance, not wanting that issue to merge in with the more
delightful one taking place then. She whimpered when his
play at her breasts ended. Her heart raced with renewed
anticipation when he ventured lower, his mouth skimming
the undersides of her plump breasts. He cupped the dark
mounds and inhaled along the curve of each. Then he was
on his way to her ribcage.

Dena brought her hands down to span the incredible width of his shoulders, the feel of the sheer power resting below her fingertips further stimulated the dull ache already thrumming to life inside the walls of her sex.

As though he sensed the need for his attention there, Carlos charted a direct course to the spot. Dena's writhing against the covers gained new life when he slowly nibbled her clit. Intermittently, he favored the satiny licorice petals of her femininity with broad strokes from his tongue.

Her breath hitched repeatedly. Her fingers at his shoulders clenched unrelentingly, his skin saved from being bloodied thanks to the worn T-shirt that hung outside equally worn denims. Aside from his nibbles and infrequent stroking, he made no move to take her with his tongue. Impatient and desire-maddened, Dena nudged his jaw with her thigh then arched her sex in a wanton display that she hoped would incite a more thorough exploration of her body. Her endeavors met with little success.

"Talk to me, babe…"

The appeal of his breath on her skin offered a hint of relief milliseconds before his verbal urgings quelled the sensation.

"Later," she refused and laughed in triumph when he gave her his tongue to enjoy.

She wanted to lock her thighs around his neck to keep him there. Instead, it was Carlos who kept her thighs locked. Securing them beneath wide palms, he permitted her few moves aside from the slight bucking of her hips. Feverishly, her inner muscles clenched around his thrusting tongue.

"Talk to me…" he murmured the request once more.

"I will…mmm…later…"

He laughed quietly, the sound muffled given his position. Tirelessly, he conducted his oral treat for a while longer- but only a short while. She moaned when he withdrew. Fists clenched, she punched at his shoulders once but firmly out of agitation.

"I told you Eva and Mae came to see me," her reminder was thick with the sobs that claimed it.

Carlos let his forehead rest on her thigh as he too worked against a fair amount of agitation. "*Why* did they come to see you?"

Breathless and hungry for the man lying just inches from where she wanted him, Dena pounded the tangled covers with a flattened hand. "They want me to help them get close to the family."

"Why?" Carlos lifted his head from her thigh. "And why would they think you'd do that?"

Dena was quiet.

"Maybe because you used to do things for them?" He finished, pretending not to feel her body going rigid over his assumption. Instead, he nuzzled into her core, kissing his way up her body until he covered her and treated her to a kiss that was laced with her need.

Drawn from her state of astonishment, Dena heartily participated in the lusty kiss until he broke it.

"Tell me what you used to do for them?"

"What do you expect me to tell you?" she sounded incredulous. This went far beyond an explanation of what prompted Evangela's and Maeva's visit.

"Carlos-"

"How about you start with Keith Bennett? I believe he was the last thing you...did for them." He ignored the widening of her deep stare. "Think it over while you get dressed." He left her in the tangle of covers.

"Come down for breakfast and we'll talk about it," he called on his way out, once again leaving his wife upright and stunned in the middle of the bed.

~CHAPTER SIX~

If anyone were to ask Dena McPhereson how she'd made it from bed, to the shower and downstairs for a breakfast she had no appetite for, she would've had no words to serve as an answer. It wasn't every day that a woman heard her husband ask about a man from her past- a man she had killed.

If he knew about Keith Bennett, what else did he know? Certainly not all of it. Bennett had indeed been her last 'job' for the Leer crew and it had been relatively... simple compared to the others. Did he know about the others?

"D! Breakfast!"

Dena's hand froze on the bannister. *The man knows when I'm coming down a carpeted staircase, chances are he pretty much knows every other damn thing I've done my entire idiotic life.* Breathing deep, she clenched the bannister and headed for the kitchen.

Dena felt her dormant appetite kick to life at the aroma of coffee, bacon and potatoes filling the inviting kitchen space. Like so many of the rooms in the cabin, the room's brick walls, throw rugs designed with a distinct Aztec flavor and stout lamps giving off rich golden light, provided a serene atmosphere whether one was chatting, eating or both.

"Eat up," Carlos suggested on his way past her en route to the dining table.

Figuring her day was bound to be an exhausting one, Dena filled a black ceramic plate with several bacon strips, a mound of the seasoned potatoes and a biscuit.

Carlos brought juice and a pot of coffee to the table before claiming his seat and preparing to dive in to the food as well. For a time, the McPheresons ate in relatively comfortable silence.

"So are big, home-cooked breakfasts, all part of the torture experience?" Dena asked halfway through the meal.

Carlos responded even as he wolfed down his mountain of food. "Do you feel tortured?"

"No," Dena ate heartily though not with the same gusto as her husband. "But there *is* a special kind of torture in being taken down a road and not reaching the logical destination."

He grinned then. The gesture accentuated the already excellent craftsmanship of his face. Dena decided to keep her eyes on her plate.

"How do you know about Keith Bennett?" she asked.

"I'm more interested in how *you* know him." He pushed aside his plate then.

The tale was not an easy one to share but Dena began as best as she could. "He was a trafficker of young women- as young as possible."

Nodding, Carlos downed a long swig of the orange juice while leaning back in his chair to observe her sharing the story.

"I didn't actually *know* him, but Evangela did." Dena ran shaking fingers across her brow and then pushed aside her unfinished breakfast.

"I met Eva Leer years ago-specifically the weekend before we broke up."

"Correction," the natural curve of his mouth grew more defined when he smirked. "It was the weekend before *you* broke up with *me*."

"I told you what happened there," she leaned closer to the table, closer to him. "I didn't tell you that I met Eva there. The things she told me- it made her sound like she'd been part of what Cufi Muhammad had started for years. I never asked how well she knew my dad and Marcus- too afraid of the answer, I guess." She covered her mouth behind her hand while considering the truth.

"Anyway, my time there was short-lived but for Eva and the rest…I guess I figured that *was* their life and I- I wanted to get back to mine." She blinked harshly as though trying to dispel sudden tears.

"I left them and went back to all my clothes and cars and Ramsey-girl status like everything that happened was just a bad dream."

"What else were you supposed to do?" Carlos voiced the challenge softly. "You didn't put them there-"

"But, Daddy-"

"*Daddy*. Not you. Keith Bennett?" He prodded when she'd kept silent for too long.

Needing something to do with her restless hands, Dena topped off her coffee and began to sweeten it. "I may not have put them there, but I still felt responsible." She left off sweetening the coffee and slammed the table with her fist.

"He was my father, dammit! He had his own daughter and he knew all those girls..." She covered her mouth again when a sob pressured her throat. "I died a little that day I walked away from you, 'Los. Hmph, a *little*- I died a lot."

"You could've told me, D. You could've leaned on me."

"I didn't want you to know what a coward I was. I didn't want to share any of that filth with you- have it touch you..." she steeled herself against slumping back on her chair. "When I finally got the nerve to leave my parents' house, I went looking for a way to help and I found Eva. She and some of the other girls had stuck together after leaving the island. I'm not sure if they left on their own or were released for being too old..." She shook her head in bewilderment.

"It was like the triangle trade or something, but in reverse- instead of heading to the new world, they were

83

leaving it for an old one where men reigned supreme and women were their slaves. I'd moved out of my folk's place, but not completely out from beneath the Ramsey umbrella. Got a job at the company in one of my father's divisions where I'd have access to funds I could use to funnel into girl's home and such. The company did that to put on the drape of caring about the community but it wasn't nearly enough. It's why Quest and Quay started their yearly endeavors to help deserving groups. They did it all above board, but I knew that sometimes you had to play foul to get good things done." She rested her elbows to the table and propped her chin on the backs of her hands.

"While I accessed all that money, I found something peculiar. Daddy was already sending out large sums of money- *off* the books. That got me even more curious since the money was going to an account in the Caymans."

Carlos made no reaction to the news though it was clear that he was riveted by the tale.

"Acting on Daddy's behalf, I was able to track down who owned that account. Eva was just paranoid enough not to leave that money in the hands of anyone but herself. It was so nice to be a Ramsey then," she smiled. "The folks at the bank were so eager to assist a member of the family who padded their establishment with so much money. They even provided me with the address of the account holder."

"And you found her?"

"The group had set up shop right there in the Caymans." Dena nodded.

"Living well off your dad's money?" Carlos guessed.

"But they weren't using it to throw beach parties. They were organizing."

He frowned. "Organizing?"

"For revenge- to take out the people who had sentenced them to such lives." She stirred the coffee she'd abandoned earlier. "Eva didn't want to tear it all down, though. She wanted to take their places at the helm."

Carlos tapped his fingers against the polished pine table. "And she needed an army to help her."

"Not an *army*- just a small crew of like-minded people."

"Like you?"

Sighing, Dena at last sipped the coffee she'd lightened and sweetened.

"Keith Bennett was a cancer like all the rest. He was responsible for shipping girls to and from the States for parties and such, overseeing transport between the island and Nice or any other properties."

"But you stopped working for the crew after that."

The coffee suddenly left a bad taste in the back of her mouth. "How did you know that? And how the hell did you know it was even me who- who killed him?"

"You were sloppy that time," he shrugged, folding his arms over his chest. "Practically signed your name to the hit. A person only leaves that kind of trail when they want to be found."

Dena had her mug poised for another sip of the coffee. Absorbing his words, she set the cup back to the table. "What do you mean? I was sloppy *that* time?" Her

ebony gaze narrowed. "Give and take Carlos," she
challenged.

He retrieved the used navy linen napkin and began
to wipe his hands again. "Hunting bail jumping idiots with
your cousin wasn't exactly my first job."

***

"Caiphus'll be pleased to know you're on board,
Bill," Lamont Pevsner gave a soft outer sigh and a deep
inner one. With any luck, he'd never have to reveal to the
lovely agent on the other side of the table that she'd already
been working for Caiphus Tesano much of her professional
career.

Sybilla pushed aside the menu she'd been studying.
"Looks like my own interests are intersecting with his once
again. And I've learned my lesson about what happens
when cases nudge ones Caiphus Tesano has already laid
claim to."

"You were all better off without that case on your
backs." Lamont said once a waiter had left to collect their
drink orders from the bar.

"How can you say that when we wound up with a
dead body to show for it?"

"Bill…"

She gave a scant wave of her hands. "I'm not
getting started, not getting started- I just wanted you to
know my plan so we can make arrangements for my team."
She passed Lamont the agent portfolio she'd brought to
their lunch meeting.

"I think Kyle Orson would be a good choice for
Team Captain." Bill smiled her thanks when the waiter

returned with the drinks she and Lamont had ordered. "The crew trusts him and he's got excellent instincts."

"I'm sure they're not as good as yours." Lamont studied the folder.

"Hmph, well we both know mine are about to be tested." Bill finished pushing a wedge of lime into her Corona. "My instincts don't seem to be as on point when I'm dealing with him."

"We'll get a meeting set to alert the team and discuss any concerns about the current case," Lamont let Bill's comment slide.

SyBilla made no indications that she'd noticed. "Looks like we're on the verge of wrapping things up. With any luck, it'll be closed within the next week or so."

"Sounds good," Lamont put the agent's portfolio to the seat of one of the unoccupied chairs at the table.

The waiter returned then for their lunch orders and silence held at the table for several seconds after the server's departure.

"You know we're about to step right back into all that mess you took us off of before," she warned her hazy stare riveted on Lamont's tanned face. "We're going to have to acknowledged how it all played in, how my family plays in…"

"Yours and Caiphus' family's involvements were one of the reasons I urged you to back off." Lamont pushed a hand through his thick hair. The gesture carried a weary overtone. "I can't have the death of another team on my hands," he sighed as if to himself and then fixed SyBilla with a rigid stare.

"Forget what Caiphus wants," he said, "this is still your choice. You don't have to give up your crew, your life to go rooting around in all this again."

"Lamont," Bill rested her hand across the cuff of his pin-striped shirt. "*This* is why I got involved in this business in the first place."

The rigid set to Lamont's attractive features softened. "I know honey," he covered her hand with his.

Bill sighed closing her eyes against the weight burdening them. "I grew up knowing there was something shady about my uncles. When I was old enough to follow my instincts, I almost got myself killed in the process." She snorted a laugh. "At least I got my answers- some of them anyway. I want to see this through, whatever the outcome."

"You know enough about who you're up against to know they'll torture you before you die if they get their hands on you." Lamont turned to face her more fully at the table. "They'll torture you SyBilla and there won't be anything you can tell them to make them stop because information isn't what they'll want from you. They'll torture you because you had the nerve to upset their plans."

He leaned in a bit closer, lowering his voice with the next words. "You were lucky with your last scrape, Bill. Ask yourself how long your luck will hold out next time and with *this* group, besides."

"Lamont what-"

Bill's attempt to question the cryptic statement was interrupted by the chiming of her boss's mobile, an effective end to the conversation.

~~~

"That him?"

"Yeah...fits the description..."

"What's the play?"

"Tail him, that's it for now. Where he goes, *we* go."

"Sounds good, so long as he keeps goin' to places with food *this* good."

There was laughter between the colleagues. One man raised his low ball glass for another hit of the bourbon he'd ordered and paused. His gaze narrowed toward the table where he and his partner held Lamont Pevsner under surveillance. The man withdrew a mobile from his breast pocket lifting a finger for quiet when his partner questioned his actions.

"Yeah, it's Baker," he said once his call had connected. "Tell the boss we've got a long dead issue that's resurfaced."

***

"I got into all kinds of trouble when you left me," Carlos told Dena later that morning over a fresh pot of coffee shared between the two of them.

"Is that why you changed schools?" She asked.

Carlos was already nodding. "My dad didn't want any of my crap getting back to the Ramseys- my folks were working for them, remember?"

Dena thought of her in-laws then. Carlos and Sherry McPhereson were both living quiet lives of retirement in their native state of Florida.

"All changing schools did was put me closer to trouble," Carlos gave a pointed sigh leaning over to brace his elbows to his knees. "But it also put me closer to people who would give me a purpose."

Dena settled deeper into the sofa warming her hands about the ceramic mug she clutched.

"I had a friend- Gram Walters- he had an uncle who was a... troubleshooter, more like a fixer. Word was, he had some high level clientele which had to be true given the way the man lived. Gram's uncle was always in the market for young blood so when Gram introduced us I was in- just like that." Carlos snapped his fingers and left the chair he'd claimed when they abandoned the kitchen for the living room.

He knelt before the fireplace to stoke still-robust flames. It suddenly occurred to Dena then that she had no real idea how much time had passed living in a house with no windows. Time had drifted by unnoticed much like the years they'd spent apart. The realization of it was all quite disorientating.

"I started with the small stuff," his pale gaze was almost olive then as it mirrored the vibrant dance of the flames he studied. "Lookouts at the docks for scheduled shipments and such- we worked in pairs. One night there was some...question about rights to a shipment that had just come in. There was a scuffle. Gram got...overzealous- a guy lost his life. Gram panicked. I didn't. I covered it up so well that Gram's uncle brought me inside his circle of advisors." Carlos laughed shortly, shook his head slightly.

"These dudes actually wanted to know what a kid like me thought and it felt good, D," he turned his head a bit more. "Felt good to be cheered instead of ridiculed. Hmph, my dad was an expert at that."

Carlos moved from the fireplace, remaining on the floor he settled back against the base of one of the armchairs. "Those old guys welcomed my actions, opinions... didn't try to make me 'get over' my rage- they welcomed it."

"They exploited it," Dena softly noted.

Inclining his head, Carlos considered the observation. "Maybe... but it felt good to be the 'good kid' for a change."

"You were *always* a good kid," Dena argued frowning stubbornly.

"But I always went against what my dad wanted," he made the confession quietly. "He never wanted us to be together, told me screwing around with you would get me locked up on some rape charge." Carlos studied his wife while reciting his father's precautions in a tone that proved he'd regarded them as pure lunacy.

"He was sure your rich folks would want their princess to marry *up*, not down. When we broke up," the energetic muscle along his jaw began to dance, "all I heard was 'told you sos' and shit... it didn't make for a nurturing home life."

Dena worked her fingers into the bunched muscles at her nape while bowing her head. To say she was sorry (again) seemed out of place yet she understood then how very much there was still left unsaid between she and her husband. They owed each other time, that was for certain but they had to use that time to fully share those aspects of their pasts that were affecting them whether they realized it or not.

"...things didn't stay so cool among my new found friends for long, either." Carlos was saying, his riveting eyes once again following the blazing fire. "Gram didn't take too well to the fact that his uncle approved of me so much. He left about two years after I joined in and wound up in places worse than any his uncle could put him. Then, he wound up on that fucking island and got himself killed for it."

Dena's resulting gasp brought Carlos' eyes back to her face.

"And *I* wound up back under your family's watchful eyes. I didn't much mind-made me feel like you were... near."

"But... how? How did that happen?" Dena's lovely features had contorted into a devastated expression.

"Remember the high end clientele Gram's uncle claimed?" He nodded once to encourage Dena to follow suit. "Two of them were Ramseys- Marcus and your dad."

Dena gave into the need to close her eyes then. Marcus and Houston Ramsey. Would the rest of her family ever be free of the corruption those two had gotten them all ensnared in?

"After I'd spent years building an expertise at handling issues of growing importance, I was called in one night for a really big job- an actual murder." Feeling that the rest of the story would require a stronger drink than coffee, Carlos went to prepare drinks at the wide bar in the corner of the room.

"Mr. Walt had tons of those over the course of any given year. Aside from that first time, *I'd* never been privy to any of the details. To this day, I don't know if that particular time was about fate dictating my chance to shine, or if it was all on purpose."

A Lover's Debt

Dena eagerly accepted the drink he provided her and hoped he didn't frown on the long swallow she took of the fragrant brandy.

"The victim was a friend of Houston's and Marc's."

The crooked smirk he sent her way would've had Dena's heart flipping any other time. Just then, it only made the muscle expand steadily blocking her throat where it lodged.

"It was all very sloppy, fingerprints everywhere." Carlos studied his brandy but didn't drink of it. "According to Mr. Walt, Marc and Houston weren't responsible-not directly. They hadn't...requested the man be killed or anything, but everybody knew he was a close associate of theirs. Then there were items found in the room to suggest the man had certain...perverse interests." He drank of the brandy then and began to pace the room.

"Marc and Houston were just trying to keep any of it from reflecting on them and their own perverse interests," he stopped and turned to face Dena then. "I'm pretty sure they didn't realize they weren't the only Ramseys being helped when they reached out to Mr. Walt and I never told my boss or anyone else that those prints belonged to you."

~CHAPTER SEVEN~

"Ethan Welch," Dena spoke the name through the shudder that made her long for something more substantial than the thin black hoody she wore. Quickly, she finished what was left of her brandy. Standing, she smoothed a hand across the seat of her faded hunter green yoga pants and crossed to the bar for a refill.

"Come sit down. Bring the bottle with you." Carlos said when she'd poured a third refill. The disbelief in her eyes when she next looked his way roused a genuine smile and he predicted her question.

"I was barely in my twenties but I had as many legal connections as illegal ones. It wasn't hard getting the prints run."

Dena was clutching a brandy decanter between her breasts. "Why did you have them run?"

"It was the Ramseys," his expression was chilling. "The two I hated and they were attached to a murder I was being told to hide. I damn well planned to have something to show for cleaning up their mess." He stared across the room as if seeing into the past.

"You were looking for something to use." She said.

"That was the plan." He stretched his denim-clad legs crossed them at the ankles. "I was going to show my father that his bosses were the true thugs, not me. I was gonna show him that wealth and a big society name didn't hide the fact that they were garbage. Then I found out those prints were yours and that-that changed everything."

Carlos rubbed his hands, one inside the other and studied the movement for a while. "I cleaned it all and went back to clean it all again after I got the report on the prints. Then I left Walt's club for good and did my damnedest to find you, but it was like you never were- like you'd just vanished."

Dena cradled the brandy as though it were a lifeline. "Ethan Welch was my first job for Eva- she threw me right in the thick of it. I guess to see if I was serious."

"Why'd you ever hook up with them?" The bewilderment in Carlos' voice echoed in his eyes.

"I needed to be doing more than I was." Her simple response was accompanied by a lost expression. "I think I just wanted to find a place to belong at first- a purpose," she gave her husband a look of understanding, recalling his earlier words to her.

"What you were doing with Houston's money- wasn't that enough?"

"Not for me." She took one hand off the bottle, pulled it through her hair. "In spite of what I knew, I...*hoped* my dad was trying to make up for what he'd done- setting up that account for Eva but in the end I knew he was trying to pay her off, buy her silence. Knowing that, I felt even less like I belonged with my family. There was a time I thought I joined up with Eva because- in a round-about way I was trying to kill myself." She drew her legs beneath her and settled back against the sofa to study the room's ceiling.

"Until that night with Ethan Welch, I never knew how much I wanted to live. He was on that insane list of hers. She's got two, you know?" Dena angled her head to send Carlos a look. "One business, one...personal," she thought of her cousin Fernando.

"I didn't know any of that at first, but now it all makes sense. She always said it was best to keep the two separate, said it was an important thing to remember, given the... things we'd have to do."

Dena straightened on the sofa, looking to the bottle clasped loosely in her hands then. "There were times when we had to-" she cleared her throat suddenly long-buried memories having their way with her emotions. "We had to get close to targets- Closer than we may've wanted to but... despite that *we* made the choice about how far to go. I didn't make the choice fast enough for Ethan and he...he wanted me to dress up for him. I did that. Then, he wanted me to perform...*with* him. I wouldn't do that. It got rough and really really ugly. He raped me."

Carlos kept his eyes downcast lest he terrify Dena with the menace lurking there. His jaw clenched as though caught in a vice so tight the muscles there were prevented from dancing their ferocious jig. All the while his hand cramped beneath the primal desire to rain down violence on the one who had savaged the woman he adored.

"After...he just laid there, but I knew he wasn't done," she used her sleeve to dab at a runny nose. "There were bottles everywhere." Carefully, she set the decanter to the floor.

"I grabbed the first one I could and hit him with it, broke it over his head and sliced up my hand in the process. He came after me," she studied her palms as if the scene were replaying itself there.

"I put the broken end of the bottle in his neck and then- just to um- just to make sure, I got the gun from my bag and I-I," she hissed a ragged breath, rubbing her palms across her thighs then.

"Eva hid me and we didn't do another job in the States for a very long time. She told me as long as I trusted her, was loyal to her no one ever had to know. I kept waiting to be caught, I was terrified but there was always a job to be done and Eva had a long list. She started with the lower level folks and worked her way up. She said it would give the higher ups time to get good and scared."

Shivering noticeably, Dena rubbed her hands up and down the thin sleeves of the hoody. "I never knew Ethan knew Marc and Daddy. Eva never told me..." she shrugged. "Maybe it's why she sent me there." She punched at the sofa.

"Such a fool- of course she knew! She did everything on purpose. Hmph...she swore she'd never go after Daddy and Marc because of me, but I never cared about that. I only never wanted you to know."

Her tears unleashed then, barely restrained with the rising discontent of her emotions. Carlos felt his own heart breaking every time her breath hitched on a remorseful sob. He went to her, lifting her from the chair and into his arms. Cradling her there, he rocked her to and fro while feathering his lips across her brow.

"I didn't want you to know this..."

"Shh...Baby shh... I would've wanted to know- would've wanted to be there."

"I didn't want that I-I did things-"

"So have I, Baby and I like to think all that shit laid the path for us to find our way back to each other." He dropped a hard kiss to the top of her head.

"Carlos-"

"Shh...hey? Enough for today, alright?" His stirring gaze narrowed as he nuzzled the softness behind her ear. "Tomorrow, okay? That's my girl," he murmured feeling her eager nod against his jaw.

Dena's sobs had quieted by the time they returned to the bedroom. Vaguely, she noted that it wasn't the room she'd been spending her nights alone in. This room was dimmer, with a more masculine feel. The bed; she realized when Carlos placed her upon it, was definitely more than twice the size of the one she'd slept in before.

Silently, Carlos berated himself. She didn't need this tonight, he thought. Not after recapping such a vicious event in her life but God... he wanted her. He roused words of calm below his breath, hoping they'd enable him to lie prone beside her; giving her comfort and taking none of what he needed from her.

Evidently, Dena disagreed. She curled her fingers into the shirt he'd changed into before breakfast. He moved to shift his weight off her. She was insistent however, lips skimming his and summoning heat instead of cool to his hormones.

"Hey," his voice was a whisper as he gently unfolded her fingers from his shirt. "We can wait."

"I *have* waited," she shifted his hold on her hands imprisoning his instead. "Love me," she pleaded, bringing his hands to her chest. Moving then, she created an arousing friction between her nipples and his palms separated only by the thin barrier of her clothing.

Regardless, the effect was stimulating and pressed her head into the king sized pillows encased in the soothing colors of gray, coral and tan. It was a rich, earthy contrast against the varied array of wooden planks that made up the walls of the room.

"You don't need this," he attempted to dissuade her even though he could barely hear his own voice above the pound of his heartbeat. "Not after telling me about that night."

Her mouth trembled on a smile, but the smile remained. "It's funny... I can't remember a thing about it now."

"D..." Carlos let his forehead rest between her breasts then, inhaling her scent and taking refuge in it. He felt her nuzzling into him, her hips enticing, inviting his to dance a timeless waltz and he knew he was done denying them both.

Once again, Dena found her fingers enveloped in his firm grasp. They were then entwined with his and being spread out from her body while his mouth worked against the rise of her breasts. The caress eased aside the fabric of the loose-fitting shirt she'd tugged on with the clinging yoga pants when she'd ventured down for breakfast hours ago. She flexed her fingers, wanting to free his hold in order to handle the removal of her attire.

Carlos seemed content with handling the task and tugged down Dena's hands to let them rest at her sides. She spasmed with the sheer anticipation of having him-really having him. He'd done it again, set her on fire for him with the uncanny finesse he possessed. The provoking enticing moves of her hips took on a needy urgency as she toiled for release grinding herself against the breath-stealing bulge that threatened to unravel the zipper of his jeans.

A wavering moan drifted up past her throat in direct response to the stabs of sensation brought on when her clit grazed his denim clad groin. A gasp chased the moan she'd uttered seconds prior when Carlos seemed to lose whatever patience he'd been fooling himself into believing he had. He freed her hands and Dena felt an instant breeze across suddenly bared breasts. She hadn't bothered with a bra and silently celebrated the choice to go without otherwise it would have met the same end as her shirt. The item was then lying in a tattered heap across the far side of the huge bed.

Carlos was cupping one of the full dark mounds, suckling with a ravenous pressure. Using his free hand, he roamed the length of her thigh until he'd hooked it beneath her knee.

His name was a chant upon her lips while she raked her nails through the close cut hair that capped his head in a crown of sleek ebony and tapered to an even line at his nape. Her fingers snaked beneath the collar of his shirt and she was desperate to have the honey tautness of his skin bared against the licorice tone of hers.

Carlos was more of a mind to dispense with Dena's clothes first it seemed. He loosed his hold on her breast to give a warning squeeze to her hand when her fingers brushed the snaps of his shirt.

"Did you bring me here for more teasing?" her words were a ragged drawl. The sound of his resulting laughter made her shiver anew.

"I thought you enjoyed my teasing," his voice was low-practically a murmur given the position of his mouth coursing the underside of a rapidly rising breast.

"Not lately," she managed to tell him.

"I'll see what I can do to change that," his laughter rumbled when she punched his shoulder.

"Teasing, teasing- I'm sorry," he hurriedly added when she poised her fist for another blow. "I love you," he vowed.

"I love you too," her eyes narrowed, "but I want this."

He plied her then with a throaty wet kiss that held every bit of the teasing element he'd apologized for only seconds earlier. For a time, he made her chase his tongue. Dena lifted her head from the pillow to take a more active role in the act. Carlos outlined the velvety softness of her mouth, dipping inside for just an instant to pay similar attention to her teeth and the roof of her mouth. All the while, he avoided her tongue which she offered to him in a desperately supplicating fashion.

She was so enamored of the erotically unorthodox kiss; that his deft removal of the rest of her clothing, went unnoticed. He was accepting her tongue as a dance partner when she groaned at the feel of her bared flesh being reawakened by the soft scrape of his worn denims.

Immediately, her legs curved about his upper thighs. She locked his perfect ass into the V of her embrace. Her kiss was hungry then, challenging him to return equal fire which he did without further resistance. Cuffing a hand about her neck, he kept her in place to accept every moist lunge of his tongue as he finally began to come out of his clothes.

Apparently feeling that he was moving too slowly, Dena offered her assistance. She ripped the snaps free and all but tore him out of his shirt. She broke their kiss then, preferring to watch the journey of her fingers across the broad plane of his chest adorned with a healthy share of intriguing scars, flexing sinews, well defined pects and abs that held her dark gaze rapt with want.

As Dena followed the trail of her fingers, Carlos drugging pale greens were fixed upon her face. He surveyed every scant change in her expression.

Of a single thought then, Dena jerked at the button clasps and zipper tab until his jeans were undone. She was then delving inside the opening of his boxers seeking the heavy organ that she could only cradle. Closing her hand around it was out of the question.

Enviably long lashes fluttering, Carlos rested his head on her clavicle happy to let her do what she would to him. Dena needed no permission and didn't wait for any. The mere promise of how incredible he would feel inside her already had her moaning her anticipation and dripping with desire for his sex.

She could feel the slow stream of her liquid need while guiding him to her core. Briefly, she tortured him by stroking his shaft's wide head up and down the folds of her love.

"Please D..."

She smiled at the sound of uncharacteristic helplessness fueling his tone as he begged her for entrance. She was overwhelmed by the love she felt- had *always* felt for the powerfully built man who lay shuddering next to her. He'd been proudly stripped of everything except his almost painful need for her.

Stillness held them willing captives once Carlos was granted the admission he craved. His big hands lay weak and half fisted against the pillows while he relished the sensuous heat and snug, creamy walls gripping him securely, anchoring him, seducing him- adoring him.

Dena released a gasping shriek when he moved inside her. Her lashes settled like hummingbird wings- his every stroke seemed to stretch her, exploring deeper and branding some part of her that had impossibly gone undiscovered by him until that moment. She noticed their hands, once again clasped and she spotted the glint of soft lighting from a far-away lamp. The illumination set upon Carlos' gold wedding band.

The colors blurred and Dena realized that her eyes were again leaking tears. The reaction had nothing to do with the sorrow that had stirred them earlier and everything to do with her devotion to the man taking her with such sweet intense care.

Carlos' hands were fully clenched into large potent fists by then one having taken hold of Dena's hand mid-flex. His mind was wiped of any thought save those of how unreal she felt, had *always* felt against him. On one accord they were as finely tuned instruments, bodies arching, bucking and swaying to a sensual refrain that never grew tiresome.

Her shrieking gasps heightened in sync to his satisfied grunts. Then he captured her hips, holding them immobile. At last, all shreds of restraint had deserted him and he pummeled her curvy frame until he poured his release deep inside her. Once spent, he maintained his hold upon her, refusing to allow her movement until he had expelled one last satisfied shudder.

Dena shuddered just as richly while tumbling over the last waves of her climax and contracted her intimate muscles around the sweet length that continued to pleasure her even as it made the transition from unyielding steel beneath honey toned silk. Carlos had just enough energy left to kick completely out of his jeans and submerge beneath the covers. There, he drew Dena into the protective unbreakable hold that echoed the strength of their bond.

~CHAPTER EIGHT~

"You just need to get back from wherever you jetted off to with your wife, else Sabra's gonna put out a search team or worse come looking for you herself."

Carlos' tall frame shook with laughter and he gave all his attention to a roaring bellow. Moses Ramsey and his wife Johari had just returned from the pre-holiday couple's getaway. Moses had spent the last half hour regaling his old friend with all the must-have, hilarious information from the trip.

Carlos' laughter was genuine. It felt good to give into the gesture and he'd been doing so with rising frequency over the last several days. He and Dena had spent the last week devoting their attention to other gestures, including but not limited to laughter. Carlos saw the woman he loved coming back to life. He never thought she could be any more beautiful than she was. He was wrong.

"So um… did you want to talk about anything else?" The easiness clinging to Moses' voice had evolved into something more solemn.

"Thanks, man," Carlos reclined against the doorframe, rubbing remnants of laugh tears from his eyes. "Nothing more than what I already told you for now. Does Pike have Belle secure?"

Moses grunted a laugh. "The man has her more secure than the President," he promised. "But you and D are alright?"

"We're good- there were things left unsaid between us. It was time to get it all out in the open and…without interruption."

"Ah-say no more," the laughter came back to Moses' voice. "Understood, but let me know if you need anything, alright?"

"You know I will. Thanks, man. I'll see you when we get home."

~~~

Dena was on her way to the kitchen when she saw Carlos emerging from a small room near the stairway that led into the bowels of the cabin. She waited for him to look up and notice her. Her heart resorted to cartwheeling when the hypnotic light stare narrowed simultaneously with the appearance of his deceptively guileless grin. Heart cartwheeling as well as thundering then, Dena thought her eardrums would explode from the pressure when Carlos closed the distance between them in the span of a few long strides.

He gathered Dena into a kiss that had her yearning to come out of her clothes. Obviously Carlos had no issue with her desire. He was already carrying her down the wide corridor, but made a detour to the kitchen where he'd planned to start breakfast following the call to Moses.

He gave Dena's bottom a few insistent squeezes, grinding her into his erection and taking pleasure in the happy moan she gave in response. He then deposited her to the counter and commenced to dining on breasts veiled by a gauzy layer of white. His mouth rooted to a nipple until it practically protruded through the fabric wetted by his bathing tongue. The long-sleeved, off shoulder top offered prime access and he had her out of it in seconds. The kitchen grew ripe with the sounds of feminine cries mingled with male groans of appreciation.

"Mmm hmm…" Dena encouraged, convulsing a little when his persuasive fingers insinuated themselves inside the cuff of the denim cutoffs she'd chosen for the day. The thick, climax-stirring digits lingered momentarily before continuing their journey into the dampened crotch of her panties.

Planting her hands on the counter space, Dena braced herself to arch up and accept as many fingers as he wanted to give her. Carlos pampered her with a devastating middle finger massage and she rocked uninhibited from the delight it produced. She heard *his* gasp and then felt his fingers working into the waistband of her shorts, tugging insistently.

"We need to eat," she reminded him coyly.

"I plan to," he grinned when he felt her shiver.

Dena felt the cool marble of the counter against her bare bottom once he'd wrenched down her shorts. Soon after, he was making good on his intention and devouring her with his tongue there on the countertop.

Her mouth was a lazy O where shaky moans drifted as her hips circled and rode the lengthy drives of his tongue. Something animalistic and distinctly male rumbled in Carlos' chest, complimented the octave of Dena's cries. Seamlessly, he hauled her up from the counter never relenting on his hungry, intimate feasting.

Dena pushed her fingers through her hair and reveled in the man's power, the total security she felt in his embrace. He supported her, loosely cradling her derriere while keeping her thighs across his shoulders, her calves hitting his back. The heart of her was open to whatever exploration he would perform on her treasure. Dena's anticipation warred with her expectancy and both enhanced her desire as Carlos carried her from the kitchen.

***

Near Invernesshire, Scotland~

"How long 'til we get to shop for baby stuff?"

Darby DeBurgh smiled at her husband through the floor length mirror where she'd stood toying with her hair.

"Shouldn't we at least wait until I'm showing? Or…I don't know…maybe until we know what we're having? Just a thought?" She sent him a wink.

Kraven DeBurgh settled himself more contentedly against the mountain of pillows supporting his back. "It's a good thought…only I may've beat you to the punch."

Sighing, Darby turned from the mirror. "What'd you do?"

"What?" A picture of innocence, Kraven continued to toss the mini soccer ball inscribed with the name of the team on his T-shirt. "I haven't done anything I'm not supposed to." He focused on tossing the ball. "I'm a father-to-be after all."

Darby could only smile at his attempt to pout.

"Anyway, it only made sense to pick up a few things while I was shopping for Quincee."

"Ha! That's good," she chuckled then, commending the man's sly attempt to combine a shopping spree for their unborn child with the one he'd launched in preparation for the pre-terrible two-party he'd given for Quincee Ramsey.

"Already over indulging in must haves for the newest addition to the DeBurgh line, tsk-tsk that's a bit obsessive milord." Darby playfully chided.

Kraven left the bed. "I actually meant to say, I picked up a few maternity clothes for you."

"Baby…" Darby could only shake her head over her husband's steadily mounting excitement. "Sweetie, I'm not even showing yet."

"Yeah…" Kraven seemed a bit too intrigued by that fact. His stirring eyes charted a slow appraisal of the black halter dress his wife had bounced around in for the better part of the day.

Darby's gaze was appraising as well and she noticed the frilly two piece lingerie ensemble he held in place of a soccer ball.

"Think you can still fit into this?"

"Well," she seemed to consider her answer. "There's really nothing to fit into." She smoothed her hands over his. "You should've brought this along on the holiday trip."

"But I-I mean- *we* could have more fun with you in it at home, don't you think?"

"Hmm…"

"I'd be very appreciative if you'd give it a try."

Darby stood on her toes. "Would you now?"

They were leaning into a kiss when the main phone line rang, filling the bedroom with its shrill cry. The lingerie was crushed between Kraven and Darby as their kiss gained fire. Regrettably, the phone's ring proved too much of a distraction.

"Kraven-"

"No."

"I'll be here after."

"But I want this now," he reached beneath her dress to cup a generous portion of her bottom. "Jesus, Darby," he moaned at the realization that she was naked underneath.

"Get the phone," she pushed at his hand.

"Where the fuck is Seamus when I need him?"

"On a well-deserved vacation." Darby said of their resident jack-of-all-trades Seamus Hale who had definitely proved his mettle when Evangela Leer and her group had come to wreak havoc.

"Why doesn't the damn thing go to voicemail?" Kraven continued to grumble while making his way across the expansive bedchamber.

Darby went back to fussing with her hair. "Seamus said it's on an extended ring in the event of emergencies."

"The man and his witty ideas," Kraven's grumbling carried even as he grinned over Seamus' precautious nature.

"It's probably Miss Moira!" Darby called, giving the name of the local tavern owner's wife. "She and Mr. Braedenton wanted us at that party for their son..."

"Charlie," Kraven supplied while pressing the phone to his ear. The main line usually carried a call from one of their neighbors in the borough.

Kraven answered good-naturedly enough, but his ease took a decided turn south the longer he held the phone to his ear. Darby noticed, turned from the mirror. She didn't have to ask what was wrong. Kraven put the phone on speaker.

"Would you mind repeating that?" He asked the caller.

"Oh uh no, no not at all Lord DeBurgh," the feminine voice on the line managed softness in spite of its high pitch. "I do apologize for the bother, Sir only the patient is rather unsettled as you could imagine."

"Oh I can imagine," Kraven's earlier ease had taken flight and he did nothing to mask his grimness.

"The poor girl is in very bad shape and in no state to talk just now, but she was found so close to the DeBurgh property...we're just hoping to find out whether anyone knows who she is."

111

Bewildered, Darby raised her hands and mouthed '*What the hell?*' to Kraven.

"What was it you said happened to the young woman?" Kraven inquired of the caller.

"Yes sir, well we hope to know more once she's had time to recover. It will be a slow road, I'm afraid. She looked like she'd been…well Sir, mauled, attacked-attacked by something monstrous."

Darby straightened her jade stare saucer-wide as she looked from the phone to her husband.

"And you say the girl had no ID?" Kraven asked.

"None, Sir, though she was dressed very well. Of course, the suit was streaked with dirt and blood but it was very easy to see that it was good material. She *was* missing a shoe, though," the woman gave a sudden twitter of laughter. "Forgive me Lord DeBurgh for prattling on."

"No need for apologies, love. I'd be very grateful if your staff would keep me posted about her condition and when she may be able to talk. I'd be pleased to help however I can."

"Oh Lord DeBurgh, how very kind…"

Darby rolled her eyes then as the woman continued to *prattle*, gushing on the line in response to the rich sing-song lilt of Kraven's voice.

"We'll make sure to keep you informed, Sir."

"I thank you for that. A good evening to you."

"Hmph, I'm guessing you can count on daily updates from here on out."

Once more, Kraven put on the face of innocence. "She only wants to be helpful, Lass."

"Oh, I'm sure," Darby laughed, but her easiness didn't hold out. "Is it one of them?" She asked.

Kraven sent a black look toward the phone. "Sounds like it."

"You think she's the only one?" Darby's hands shook and she clutched them while drawing nearer to Kraven. "Do you think the rest might be around somewhere- lurking?"

"Christ," Kraven rolled his eyes silently chastising himself for upsetting her. He pulled his wife into a crushing hug.

"Should we tell the others?" Darby's words were muffled in the base of his throat.

"No Lass, no… Fern looked good during the trip but he could still use more time to get back to normal after what happened."

Darby nodded, breathing in Kraven's calm-inducing scent as she kept her face against him.

"We'll let them know when we have to."

Darby shuddered again. "*When*, not *if?*" She pointed out.

"Shh," he gave her a squeeze then drew his fingers up through her hair and tugged a little. "We're fine, Lass. We're fine."

***

"After what happened that night, I knew I wasn't cut out to be one of Eva's 'Black Widows," Dena's laughter was weak but the sound was fueled by humor albeit short-lived.

Shivering against a scant chill, Dena snuggled back into Carlos' warmth in the bed where they'd returned

113

following the seductively charged scene which began in the kitchen and culminated in the hallway just outside the living room.

"Eva wasn't having it," Dena rested her head on one of Carlos' biceps relishing the contentment instilled by his breadth and hardness.

"She didn't abide by quitters and she praised loyalty- told me the disloyal were no better than the trash we were taking out of the world." She snorted at the concept. "So I believed her bullshit and I stayed- convinced myself that I owed them for what my family helped to put them through."

Carlos skimmed his mouth across her shoulder and Dena took refuge in the escape provided by the simple caress. She could have dwelled there endlessly, but resisted the urge to hide in that cocoon of tenderness.

"The um...the work helped me to forget," Dena pushed up to sit amidst the tangle of bedcovers. "I guess there was *some* payoff but then that only helped when I was on the job..." She hugged herself. "At night, the second I closed my eyes, there were these dreams, the most awful dreams," Dena drew her knees up to her chin and huddled near the headboard.

"I'd had them for years along with headaches that started after the *family trip* with Daddy and Marc."

Still laying back in the bed, Carlos worked the heels of his hands against his eyes. The ill-fated trip had prefaced the end of their relationship and brought about the injury that cast down any hope of them ever conceiving a child together.

114

"...the dreams and headaches usually came 'round anytime I saw Sheila." Dena referenced Carlos' sister.

"I was sure to have one anytime Taurus or the guys even mentioned *your* name." She glanced in his direction, but didn't look at him fully.

"They were bad, but after that night with...Welch, they were debilitating and I-I probably couldn't have held down a real job if I'd tried," she shrugged. "At least working for Evangela and company paid well and she even knew how to make the pain stop."

Carlos pushed himself up slowly amidst the covers.

Dena didn't need eye contact to read the question sharpening his appealing features. "There was something she'd give Maeva- to help her cope- ReGen," Dena sighed the name of the drug she'd once considered her savior. "It became my lifeline. I almost couldn't function without it." She buried her face in her hands and groaned.

"The damn stuff wasn't even manufactured to be a drug," she muttered, "it was a by-product, some kind of ingredient they used in experiments or something. Eva never gave any specifics about it- not that I asked," she laughed then. "She could've paid me with ReGen instead of money and I'd have been satisfied." She bristled, resisting Carlos' touch when he inched closer.

"It kept me in a haze, but with it I could carry out all the depraved duties Eva required of her small staff and I handled my duties with great enthusiasm." She looked at him then, wanting him to see the ugly truth of her words when they reflected in the shadow of her stare.

"I staked out Keith Bennett that night," she let her eyes falter from his mesmerizing pale stare to rest on the bedcovers. "He was being interrogated by the people Bill worked for."

"Bill?" Carlos repeated the name of Dena's cousin SyBilla Ramsey.

Dena nodded. "Eva's connections are unreal. She's got as many legal connections as illegal ones."

"Hmph," Carlos recalled making the same boast with regard to himself.

"Bill still has no clue that her own boss is under Evangela's wingspan. I don't know if she'll ever forgive me for not telling her that. Lamont Pevsner got himself...caught up in things like I did- it may be why I kept his secret when he asked me to." She gave a pointed sigh. "Anyway, Bennett was there being questioned and so I waited. Eva fixed it to have him released. She'd been after him for a while and I never knew if he was on her business or personal list."

Dena smiled sadly. "Whatever the reason, she wanted him dead and I didn't care given what I knew of the man. But when he saw me," she hid her face that time in the sheet, inhaling deeply several times to stifle a heightened flash of emotion.

"When he understood why I was there, standing outside the car he'd driven to the pier where I followed him...he begged." She shook her head, eyes set across the room as though she were seeing the scene she described.

"He sat there behind that wheel and cried like a child, saying he was sorry and-" she let her hands fall to her lap in a helpless display. "All those tears got to me I guess. I um, all that time I waited outside for him to be released...I don't know...maybe my head started to clear a little- not enough for me to be totally forgiving. I *did* kill him after all."

"I don't know what made me get in his car, but I sat on the passenger seat and just watched him for- I don't know...long enough for me to leave behind too many fingerprints and my clutch piece," she leaned back her head and smiled. "Then, I just had to go and vomit all over the dashboard."

"Like I said, 'sloppy'," Carlos' soft-spoken words carried playful sarcasm.

"But I'd had enough," Dena nudged his shoulder with hers. "Not even an unlimited supply of that fucking drug could change that. Eva didn't try to stop me though. Guess she figured I'd come slouching back when coming down off the ReGen was more than I could handle.

"I called Taurus. He was in law school by then, but he dropped everything and took care of me. Got me settled in the States, helped me find a job." She suddenly laughed a genuine laugh. "It was a normal, drama-free job too."

Carlos risked touching her then, smiling when she didn't retract from his fingers on her cheek. "T's a good guy," he said.

"He's the best," her nod was decisive. "He wouldn't let our family's crap touch me. He did his best to keep me sheltered even though he was aching to talk to someone about everything going on in his own life." Her eyes went blurry then and her lip trembled against the sob pressuring it.

"*I* was the oldest, dammit. I should've been the one taking care of *him*!"

"Hey?" Carlos took her by the hands then, tugging her around to face him. "It wasn't your fault- none of it."

"But somebody had to take responsibility no matter whose fault it was." Dena drew the back of her hand across the chords of muscle defining his chest.

"I wasn't in any shape for it back then," she curled into the pillows when Carlos released her. "So I lived my life quietly and it was okay. If I could've made it without you, I would've probably lived out my days never thinking of that. I could've done it had it not been for Taurus' call about five years ago."

"Sounds ominous," Carlos noted, idly brushing his thumb along the bend of Dena's elbow.

"Not really," she smiled. "His voice sounded… different. Not bad, not happy exactly…but something had turned on a light inside him."

"Nile," Carlos guessed.

"It wasn't an 'in love' kind of sound," Dena bit her lip on a smile, remembering how aggravatingly giddy her little brother was when he met his future wife. She smiled for a time, thinking of the couple.

"No this was something else and Taurus was calling it Michaela Sellars."

"Mick?" Carlos laughed a bit, pushing himself up against the pillows then.

"He told me she was a writer interested in chronicling the family's history. 'Course *he* was more interested in discussing her looks and griping about how Quest had already staked a claim."

Carlos dissolved into a rumble of laughter, while Dena smiled over the old memories. The joy they stirred took root for only a moment or so.

"Taurus told me how upset Daddy was about Mick being there, asking all those questions about Sera." Dena thought of the young woman who had been murdered by her father while his brother looked on. Hmph... upset... Taurus said he was livid." She clutched a fistful of the covers and then smirked. "T said it was something to see the great Houston and Marcus Ramsey riled by a little thing like Mick.

"It all made sense then." Dena flexed her toes beneath the covers as though the memories had suddenly rendered her restless. "All those calls I started getting within weeks of Mick's arriving in Seattle. I told Daddy to stop calling me, but he didn't- they were actually kind of nice-the calls...made me think about how we used to be before-"

"Let's stop," Carlos suggested, seeing his wife's unease and then favoring her temple with a light kiss when she shook her head.

"They seemed innocent- the calls. He'd want to talk about how I was living, if I had any new friends. If I had... any new friends wanting to discuss family business- family secrets. And I knew...

"I don't know how, but I...I knew what happened to Sera wasn't an accident. I guess I always knew it but he was my dad and I told myself that he couldn't possibly...I believed all that guff they rammed down our throats about it being an accident. She was my best friend, like a little sister- one I'm glad I never had because she would've ended up just like me."

Her laughter held a wildness and she kicked at the sheets covering her feet. "She ended up much worse than I did though and my own father was to blame." The tension in her shoulders eased off when Carlos' mouth grazed her shoulder. The gesture summoned calm at once.

"I took a closer look at what happened to me then. Daddy didn't care. He just didn't want it to come back and bite him and Marc, but he never cared about what any of it did to me. He only cared about what Marcus said, what Marcus did, thought... the money he was doling out to Eva was just a payoff. It had nothing to do with redemption or remorse."

"But why them?" Carlos asked, his brow furrowed, "why were *they* paying? And why tap Houston's pockets? What about Marc's?"

"Why pay for your own crimes when you can have a gullible little brother handle his and yours too? Besides, they weren't the only ones. Eva tapped lots of pockets. The thing with making lots of money is that you can never make enough and sometimes the most profitable ways aren't the most moral."

Though she was well within touching distance, Carlos didn't care for Dena being even that far away. He pulled her back against him in one easy move, locking her in the shelter of his arms and rocking her slow.

"I put myself in the lion's den," she said. "Trying to make up for what they did- for what I heard in my dad's voice when he called- it told me they were *still* doing it."

She turned into Carlos then, indulging in the warmth stirred from the friction of their bare bodies.

"I knew I couldn't repay anything living the life Eva wanted for me, but I couldn't repay anything by hiding either."

Carlos nudged her chin with his fist. "You've got nothing to repay, D. You need to understand that."

Her smile was a sad one. She uncurled his fist and pressed a kiss to his palm. "I heard that fear in Daddy's voice," she kept his hand between her breasts and rested her head on his chest. "I heard how scared he was of whatever Mick would find researching the family for her book and I thought- this could be it." She clenched a fist then.

"I thought that maybe if I threw my support Mick's way, others would too- they'd realize the tide was turning and maybe the evil duo would start answering for their actions."

"That's a lot of hope to put on a book," Carlos said.

"You're right," Dena puffed out her cheeks in preparation for a heavy sigh. "But it wasn't so much the book as what the book represented. The book meant questions-questions about Sera. Hers was a case everybody knew was handled badly and overlooked because- well… she was Sera Black and we were the Ramseys."

Dena clenched her fist again and gave it a little shake. "I knew Mick would find the truth because that was her job and then she met Sera's mother and it became her mission to give that woman closure."

She thumbed a tear from her eye. "You say I don't have a debt to repay? That I don't owe anything because of

121

what my father and uncle did to me and my cousins? You may be right, but I damn sure owe one to Mick. Her presence was the kick in the pants I needed to pull my head out of the sand. She made me care that the world knew we weren't a bunch of wealthy snobs who thought we were above the law. That was only Houston and Marc.

"She gave me hope in the most far-fetched things, like maybe one day I'd have you back," she grazed a lazy kiss across one of his biceps smiling when he flexed a muscle in response.

"I hoped that I-I'd be good enough for you again," her smile wavered a bit before she pressed her lips together.

Carlos surrounded her in the fortress-like shelter of his embrace. "You were never anything less to me," he made her lie prone against him. "I never want you to think that you could ever be less and I damn well never want to hear you say it." He kissed her forehead, stunned to feel his eyes pressuring with tears then.

"I never will," Dena vowed, clutching him as tightly as she could. "I never will."

~CHAPTER NINE~

"Are you saying she could die?" Darby studied the waif-thin redhead in disbelief.

Dr. Leti Bobbin fixed the devastating couple before her with an empathetic sky blue gaze. "This is very frustrating. We'd hoped the patient would be moving closer to recovery by now, but sadly it appears just the opposite. There's an internal bleed that we've been unable to stop. If things don't improve, chances are great that we may lose her. Any information you might provide could prove most helpful. We'd like to get word to her family ASAP."

Darby bristled then, almost feeling the angry vibrations searing the fuzzy gold wool of her sweater. A sound closely resembling the churn of an idling motor stirred from Kraven's chest as he stood behind her.

"Doctor we um, we really aren't sure we know your patient at all. We did some...entertaining a while back and she *may have* been among the guests. Until we see her..." Darby spread her hands to emphasize her point. "We can't be sure since you've yet to determine her identity."

"Yes, yes of course." Dr. Bobbin nodded, her brilliant red tresses a vibrant contrast against her alabaster skin. "She's a bit groggy-we've been trying to keep her sedated. Rest is all we can give her now."

"I understand," Darby smiled.

"I'm not sure you do, Lady DeBurgh, Lord DeBurgh," the doctor's voice softened more noticeably when she addressed the darkly imposing man who had yet to speak.

"Doctor Bobbin, it's Kraven and Darby," Darby corrected with a kind smile.

"Certainly," the woman bowed her head and gave it a quick, singular shake. "It's not often that royalty walks into our quaint little clinic."

The Mogey Clinic had been fashioned from an old parsonage as a clinic to service the area's vast community of elderly farmers. It was a demographic who either had little trust of big city hospitals or lacked the transportation and funds to travel there.

Dr. Bobbin's eyes had repeatedly traveled toward Kraven. Finally, the efficient doctor gave up all hope of looking elsewhere and locked in on the man's face for a time.

Darby allowed the woman a few moments to oogle her husband who; despite his obstinate scowl, could do little to douse a woman's interested once she saw him.

"The uh, the young woman has gone into a kind of delirium," Dr. Bobbin at last regained a handle on her professionalism. "She keeps talking about someone dying. At first, we thought she was talking about herself but it sounds like she needs to warn someone. We thought it might be a family issue hence our efforts to try retracing her steps." Clasping her hands, the doctor scanned the clinic's lobby with a loving but scrutinizing gaze.

"We've a good clinic, but ill-equipped for the major surgeries which may save her life. Unfortunately, moving her to another location might do more harm than good."

In many ways, Darby thought. Silently, she pondered the certainty that the injured woman was one of Evangela Leer's team. Should Dr. Bobbin's patient want to *warn* someone of impending death, that may be major cause for Evangela to; as the doctor put it, 'do more harm than good'.

"Could we see her, Doctor?" Darby asked.

"Yes, yes, certainly," Leti Bobbin waved her hands and began a retreat towards the clinic's front desk. "Let me just check in quickly with the nurses."

Dr. Bobbin headed for the small red oak station in the far corner of the lobby. The establishment could have easily doubled as a cozy bed and breakfast. Sadly, the clinic's calming powers had yet to rub off on Kraven. Darby turned to address her husband, already raising her hands in a gesture meant to incite peace.

"So I'll just go in and you can wait-"

125

"Bugger that shit!"

Darby yanked the hem of the metallic gray hoody Kraven wore and pulled him to the other side of the lobby. There, she tried to reason with the man who studied her as if she were a child he was losing patience with.

"The woman is bed-ridden. She's no threat, *and-"* she stressed when Kraven opened his mouth to refute her words. "She's probably not going to share much with you snarling down at her." Looking past him, Darby saw the doctor approaching. She bumped her fist to the center of Kraven's chest.

"If I'm gone more than an hour, send in the dogs," she pacified him with a kiss, pushed him into a seat that groaned in protest of his weight, and headed off to meet with the doctor.

~~~

Dr. Bobbin ushered Darby into the small room where a woman lay beneath a pile of covers on an elevated twin bed.

"I'll just give you some time alone," the doctor tipped from the close, dim room.

Alone, Darby used her mobile to snap a picture of the unidentified woman whose face had thankfully escaped the dogs' affections.

"Hello?" Darby wasn't necessarily expecting a response to her greeting and nearly fell off her feet when she got one.

"They're gonna kill her. They- they found her- her and they're gonna-"

"Hey? Shh…shh…" Darby glanced over her shoulder, not ready for the doctor's return. Darby flinched when the woman stilled suddenly, appearing completely lucid when she looked her way.

"Dena? Dena." The woman inquired.

***

Queens, New York~

"I told Rena she didn't have to bother you." Gabriel Tesano stood from the chair he'd occupied since the housekeeper had gone to get his brother.

Aaron Tesano cleared the last of the steps from the rear stairs that led into his den. "I try to get out of bed for a few hours every day anyway," he told his younger brother.

"How you doin'?" Gabriel asked, nodding in reference to the quick health re-cap Aaron supplied.

"I know you didn't just drop in to check on me, Grekka?" Aaron tacked on to his health report.

"I um," briefly Gabriel massaged his jaw. "I was at the cemetery. Spent most of the day at Giselle's and Brogue's graves."

The explanation gave Aaron pause. The cemetery to which Gabriel referred was located not far from Aaron's brownstone. The Grove Cemetery served as the resting place of every Tesano that had come to the New World from the old.

"You want a drink?" Aaron offered. "I could have Rena-"

"She already took care of me," Gabriel reached for the bourbon and rocks he'd placed on the high end table next to the chair he'd taken while he waited.

127

"The wench told me she threw it all out," A wry smile enhanced Aaron's dark olive-toned face.

"She's just lookin' out for you," Gabriel grinned.

"So she tells me," Aaron gave an acknowledging smile and then went to the small fridge behind the bar and selected from an array of juices and iced teas. He popped the cap on a bottle of cranberry juice and then rejoined his brother in the sitting area.

"My heart goes out. Losing Brogue...I know it was beyond hard."

"I never wanted this for him, Ari," Gabriel downed a healthy portion of his drink. "I know you think I'm full of shit, but I honestly never did."

"I know that, Grek," Aaron raised his glass in a mock show of understanding. "I've never been a father but it's something I choose to believe."

"Why didn't you ever take the vows, Ari?" Gabriel asked once he'd considered Aaron's words.

"Wasn't strong enough to deal with what our family might do to the woman I loved," Aaron's response was firm and unapologetic.

Gabriel smirked, regarding his drink but not sipping. "Wish I'd have thought of that before I brought Giselle home."

"Hmph, she was tough. Turned us all to puddy in the palm of her hand." Aaron mused, his handsome rugged features softening over the memory of the woman.

"Humphrey was the worst," Gabriel noted, joining in when Aaron laughed. "Why do you think that was?" He asked, sobering a little.

Aaron was still caught up in his laughter. "Because she was a damn beauty, that's why." He studied the light filtering the glass of cranberry juice and smiled. "I spent many a day concocting a way to steal her from you myself."

"Hump always acted like he was trying to solve a riddle when he looked at her- like he was trying to figure her out."

"Because she was a damn beauty..." Aaron sang once more as if to prove his point.

"Maybe," Gabriel's light blue stare harbored scant traces of doubt. "I think that's why he never really let me into his inner circle."

The uncommon ease Aaron felt in his brother's company began to wane. "Inner circle or not, they're coming and you're damn well in their sights."

Gabriel finished off his drink. "I expect nothing less," he said.

The admission surprised Aaron and it showed.

"I'm not here for sympathy or mercy, Ari," Gabriel set aside the empty glass. "Standing over Brogue and Giselle today I-I understand why I lost Brogue, but never Giselle. I've never understood that, never gotten past it." He hunched forward, elbows resting upon trouser clad knees. "Maybe if I had, I wouldn't be the villain our brothers and nephews want to kill."

"If it makes you feel better, you're not alone." Aaron's voice was mockingly hopeful. "Vale's right in the bulls-eye with you." Silently, Aaron noted that their brothers and nephews had a more personal loathing for Gabriel given his role in Imani's injury.

129

"They may want to give Vale the benefit of a chat before they send him to his death." Gabriel cautioned. "If they're serious about tearing all this down, the family business is just a small part of it."

"We know about the island."

Gabriel didn't seem unnerved by the news. "The island's a bigger piece, but not the heart of it."

"So why don't you stop fucking around and tell me what is?"

"Because the fact that Black Island isn't the heart of it all is *all* I know." Gabriel spread his hands in a defeated manner. "Vale's running it though, same as he is the island."

"Vale?"

Gabriel smiled. "Ari, I haven't been superior to our little brother since Hump died. He wanted Vale to succeed him." He slumped back in his chair. "It's a funny thing because V never even believed in Humphrey's philosophies. He believed in the wealth that philosophy would generate and so long as the profits are up to par, the means of obtaining them run unchecked- no matter *how* corrupt they are." He leveled a guarded look at his brother. "To this day, I believe it was that corruption that took Giselle from me."

"Grek," Aaron closed his eyes. "Giselle wouldn't have wanted you obsessing over her loss after all these years-"

"Just hear me out Ari? Please?"

Aaron shrugged, loosening the robe's belt at his waist. "Why me?" He challenged.

Gabriel burst into quick laughter. "Do you really think they'll give me a chance to open my mouth for any other reason than for them to put a gun in it? They aren't going to let me talk."

"And *why* are you talking? After all this time?"

Gabriel slanted a fleeting look to his empty glass and sighed. "I've done what I've done and I'm ready to accept the consequences for it. Maybe if I'd had this sudden epiphany long ago, I could've put my boy on a better path and he'd be alive today. Maybe Giselle would be too and I would've been a man who would've deserved a girl like her."

"Grek-"

"You know it's true, Ari-" Gabriel eyed his brother with playful suspicion. "All that teasing about taking her from me, it was true. Wasn't it? You loved her."

Aaron wouldn't answer. He didn't have to since the truth of Gabriel's words lurked in his dark, deep-set stare. "I'm an old man, Grek," he responded finally. "Exactly what is it you expect me to do?"

"Just listen to me," Gabriel extended a hand. "What little I know might help them later. They'll destroy it all one way or another. I know they will. I stuck my head in the sand and let Vale run things his way after Hump died. Hmph, what did *I* care when the ass didn't even trust me to be in charge? He told me once that I was a lover and not a businessman..." Gabriel nodded as if accepting the charge.

"I know you think I'm talkin' a lot of bunk, Ari. Maybe I am, but it could help when it's time to go after Vale. Promise me you'll remember that."

Aaron nodded once a full minute had passed. "You have my word," he said.

***

"Anything?" Evangela asked Saffron when the woman joined her that night on the balcony outside her private parlor.

"Nothing. Thanks," Saffron took a seat on the rocker Evangela motioned her toward. "You know we may have to entertain the possibility that she might be dead."

Evangela didn't rage over the woman's carefully spoken observation. Instead, she appeared weary- weary and exhausted.

"Dammit Cas," she sighed, rubbing her hands against the gray chiffon sleeves of her lounging dress. "You know, I could always count on her for the truth. Hmph, whether I wanted it or not. Cas always gave it to me straight and how'd I repay her? By trying to choke the life from her."

"Cas knew you loved her," Saffron's locks bumped her long oval face when she shook her head.

"I did-I swear I did." Evangela studied the sky for an extended moment. "She was my confidant. Cas was the confidant I hoped, *expected* Dena to be. Stupid, I was," she berated herself then smiled at Saffron. "Sharing blood with someone does *not* make them a soul-mate.

"That was Casper," she said once she and Saffron shared easy laughter. "We told each other our secrets," she began to rock her chair. "Things I never told anyone else. Ha! *So* much I can't remember half of it. We have to find her, Saf," her voice held a resolved tone then.

132

"If she's alive," Saffron continued to speak carefully, "she may be too injured to make her way back to us. The longer she stays put, the better her chances of being found."

"If that's the case, if Cas is somewhere and can't be moved, we'll be sure to take her out of her misery when we find her." Evangela continued to rock her chair, all traces of despair dissolving. "She'd rather die than betray me."

***

"Thank goodness for tinted windows," Dena was removing her jacket while Carlos got settled behind the wheel of the Suburban. "This snow is blinding."

"It's probably snowed every day and night since we've been cooped up in that place." Carlos set a sidelong glance toward the cabin.

Dena observed the dwelling with not nearly the amount of abhorrence she'd had upon their arrival. Smiling serenely, she turned back to Carlos leaning over the gear shift to brush a kiss across his cheek.

"I liked being cooped up with you," she spoke the words against his mouth.

"Did you like all of it?"

"Yes," she confirmed without hesitation. "Sitting here with you now on the other side of it all. Yes I did."

"Can I ask you something?" She watched as he started the SUV's powerful engine.

"Anything."

Despite her anxiety, Dena took a moment. "Overall, did you really think I was a... sloppy assassin?"

Carlos laughed heartily. "What?" He asked while setting the heating gauge.

"After that first time," she wiggled her fingers before the air vent, smiling as the strong rush of warmth met her skin. "I tried to be more careful. I didn't want to wind up in jail and Evangela was a stickler for excellence. If you were anything less, you damn well learned to shape up quick. You finding Bennett that way-you weren't tracking all my jobs or...were you?"

Carlos was resting back against the driver's seat then. The set of his stare proved that he sensed his wife's concerns. If her- sloppiness had led him to her, what would stop anyone else? Specifically, what might stop any authority who might want to see her pay for her crimes?

"No babe. After Welch, I didn't catch a whiff of anything you'd done," he leaned across the gear changer, freed a lock of hair from its provocative hiding place inside her sweater. "It's like I said before. You just vanished."

"But how did you find Bennett?"

"There was a bounty on him," Carlos set his elbow on the driver's side rest. "That's how I hooked up with Mo. I'd just visited Sheila. She was working for that asshole Stef Lyons."

Dena shivered a bit, recalling Fernando's deceased business partner and one of Marcus Ramsey's budding list of crazed illegitimate offspring.

"Sheila was talking about Fernando as usual," Grinning, Carlos thought of his sister's long-time crush on the man. "Anyway, the conversation shifted to his brothers and then she was telling me about the business Moses had started.

"I called Moses-figuring my... skill set would be useful."

"And it's been a long, happy relationship ever since?"

Carlos' smile illuminated the appeal of his stirring eyes. "We've had our ups and downs but yeah- he's a hell of a guy. I've never regretted working for him."

"Was Bennett your first case together?"

"We handled a couple of earlier ones before the Bennett hunt showed some teeth. Keith Bennett was another with a knack for falling off the radar. When he *did* surface, he was being questioned in connection to a drug bust."

Dena turned the information over in her mind. "Eva never gave us much reason for *why* we were going after some of the folks she targeted. We only knew that they were connected to the island. Had I known that Fernando-"

"Hey? Shh…" he shook his head, already taking note of her rising guilt. "No."

He kissed her nose and she nodded. "No taking blame," she acknowledged the rule.

They were about to kiss again when the sound of an old fashioned telephone ring filled the SUVs cabin.

"Back to the real world," Carlos grumbled and grabbed his mobile from the dash. "Speak of the devil," he chuckled, slanting a wink to Dena while pressing the phone to his ear. "Moses!"

Dena tossed her cuffed fleece jacket to the back seat, and then dug out her IPod while Carlos handled the call with her cousin. She was scrolling a playlist to set the tone for their drive when she tuned in to her husband's voice adopting a decidedly darker octave. When a few choice obscenities were added to the conversation, she forgot about choosing music and waited.

Carlos ended the call, but not before he tapped the mobile's faceplate and studied what appeared on the screen.

"What?" Patience depleted, Dena slapped his arm. "What'd Moses want? Did everybody get back from the trip okay?" She referred to the couple's getaway the group had enjoyed back east.

"Is it Belle? Did Eva-"

"She's fine, she's fine," Carlos gave her hand a few reassuring pumps.

"Then what?" Dena fidgeted like a restless child against the seat.

"Moses got a call from Kraven a few hours ago. Looks like one of Evangela's crew is still nearby in Scotland."

"Are Kraven and Darby okay? Did something happen?"

"That's not it, the woman's in a clinic close to Kraven's place. He and Darby went to see her. She asked for you."

Dena flinched, her hand going limp inside Carlos'.

He turned the mobile so that she could see the screen. "Do you know her?" He asked.

It took Dena some time to look away from Carlos and focus on the mobile screen. She frowned, inclining her head a fraction before she took the phone away from him.

"This is Casper. Casper M'Baye."

~CHAPTER TEN~

Portland, Oregon~

Following Moses' call and photo attachment, the McPheresons shifted their plans to return to Seattle. Content with the items they'd packed for the cabin, they took the ninety minute drive from Mt. Hood to Portland. Along the way, Dena had secured flight plans out of PDX Airport to Scotland.

Carlos and Dena arrived with two hours to spare before departure. They used the opportunity to settle down in one of the cozy pubs the hub boasted.

"Brandy will do the same things chamomile will, you know?" Dena chimed in once Carlos had placed the order. The Brandy was for him.

"Clutching a warm mug might help those shaky fingers of yours," he noted with a sly wink.

Dena clenched her hands, hiding them under the small table they'd grabbed close to the bar area. She hadn't even felt the trembles that his keen vision had spotted. "I could've used you looking over my shoulder back then." She confessed, staring idly at the busy bar workers servicing visiting travelers.

"No place else I would've wanted to be," he said.

"Then why didn't you come find me?" Dena countered, the smallest hint of a frown sharpening her soft features. "You never came to find me. Not even after Bennett."

The server returned with their drinks and Dena relaxed in the surprisingly comfortable ladder backed chair.

"I hope you'll be staying long enough to dine with us tonight?" The waitress inquired.

Dena caught the whiff of subtle flirtation unmistakably directed at her husband and she smiled. The server balanced her tray surprisingly well given that her lips were parted as though she were panting and her eyes intently chased Carlos' every move.

Before their episode at the Oregon hideaway, Dena almost believed her husband was oblivious to his appeal. She'd often wondered whether he picked up on even a hint of the attention he beckoned when he entered a room.

She could feel her hands shaking then. Not out of unease, but with a driving desire to explore the sinewy perfection that so many pairs of hungry eyes in the pub were envisioning beneath the coconut brown corduroy shirt he wore.

"You want something, D?" He was asking, smiling encouragingly as if he had no idea he was being mentally undressed by at least two women.

"Could you come back in a few minutes?" Dena asked the waitress.

"That's no problem at all," the woman gave Carlos the answer but quickly favored Dena with a polite smile. "Enjoy your tea," she said before hurrying off.

"Holly Springs, North Carolina," Carlos said.

Dena straightened, hands resting flat on the square table then. Swallowing noticeably, she bowed her head while recapping their abundant conversation over the last several days. In all they'd shared, she couldn't recall telling him where she'd lived.

"How-"

"You vanished again after Bennett." Carlos turned the brandy snifter in a circle on the napkin beneath it. "But by then, I was working with Moses and that gave me more time with your family. Your mom always liked me, you know?"

Again, Dena smiled at the man's cluelessness. Silently, she recapped the many instances she'd caught the late Daphne Ramsey eyeing her daughter's young boyfriend with a mix of motherly adoration and womanly lust.

"She did. She really did." Was all the confirmation Dena dared give. Her husband's honey-toned face would flush burgundy if she told him how much her mother actually liked him.

"I had the chance to see a lot of Taurus. He was always real sympathetic given what he knew about our breakup." He left the glass alone and watched her for a moment.

"One day he tells me that you want me to live- not spend my time regretting…and to not worry because you were fine. I don't know," he shrugged and worked a hand over the light shadow already darkening his jaw. "Something in the way he said it… probably a long shot, but I thought what the hell. I checked into your little brother's travel schedule and found out he made quite a few trips to N.C. Nowhere near where he was in school."

"Why didn't you-?"

Carlos was already shaking his head on her question. "You were working for their cultural center, is that right?" He watched her nod dazedly. "The place was good for you. I saw the girl I loved in that place."

"And you never told anyone you knew?"

"Played the role like I had no clue," his tone was quieter. "I found more than your prints when I found Keith Bennett. Connections to a ship- The Wind Rage."

Dena's jaw dropped and she was glad for the heated mug against her chilly palms. The Wind Rage was owned by Cufi Muhammad AKA Charlton Browning and his old friend Marcus Ramsey.

"We uncovered more and more and I insinuated myself deeper and deeper into that world," he drank deeply of the brandy then. "It was sick, but I stayed-weaved myself in so deep, I was offered the chance to work for the organization."

Needing a sudden hit of calm, Dena drank more than half of the fragrant tea.

"Moses agreed that working undercover would get us info we would've never been privy to," his uncommon stare softened while caressing every inch of her face. Mo was determined to find out what had happened to Zara," Carlos referred to his old friend's deceased sister-in-law. "He was obsessed with it, trying to redeem himself for Johari," he referred to Moses's wife then.

"I knew you were in North Carolina with T looking out for you. I couldn't walk away then," his voice became a whisper and he shook his head. "Not when everything I'd been working on since... forever kept leading me back to your family or you. Since the day I lost you, I've been trying to find out why. I chose satisfying my curiosity over being with you."

Suddenly, Carlos pressed the back of his hand across his eyes. He seemed stunned by the moisture that had pooled there. Tears were already brewing in Dena's eyes.

"Do you forgive me, D? Will you? For wasting all that time?"

The water streamed her lovely dark face then and she exchanged her chair for a seat in his lap. Kissing his temple hard, she let her mouth linger there. They rocked against each other, absorbing the truth and the burdens it lifted.

***

Edinburgh, Scotland~

The DeBurghs were on hand to greet the McPheresons upon their arrival. Once hugs and handshakes were out of the way, Carlos and Kraven went to retrieve the baggage while Dena and Darby followed along at a slower pace.

"Sorry your first trip has to be under these kinds of circumstances." Darby relayed her apologies while she and Dena walked arm in arm.

"I wanted to know," Dena nudged Darby's shoulder with her own. "Still doesn't make me eager to see the woman- if that makes sense."

Darby's emerald stare narrowed when she laughed. "It makes perfect sense," she gave Dena's arm a pat and the two rushed to catch up with their husbands.

From the airport, the group took a short drive to the Muir Inn where Kraven kept a split level suite. He had secured similar accommodations for Carlos and Dena, figuring the couple was entitled to at least *one* night of relaxation before opening the doors to another domain of hell.

The allure of the five-star inn called to both couples the moment they arrived. With check-in procedures already handled, there was no need to visit the glossy oak front desk.

The group made their way across the lobby's beige and crème checkerboard flooring. En route to the elevator bay, they passed the mahogany suede sofas intermingled with deep almond colored armchairs. With digs secured on the same floor, Kraven and Darby urged their guests to rest and planned to meet them in a few hours for a late supper.

The classic architecture and rich, earthy tones of the throw pillows and blankets were unarguably striking. Carlos and Dena however were most impressed by the bed. Quietly, they selected their sides and removed their shoes in a comfy silence. The simple actions drained what little energy they had. In moments, the two were tumbling down to snuggle their heads into the pillows and lose themselves in sleep's deep well.

~~~

Carlos woke little over an hour before he and Dena were to meet Kraven and Darby for dinner. Carlos left his wife sleeping and headed for the shower. When he returned, he found Dena standing in the balcony that offered them a stunning view of the inn's rear property facing out toward a dense forest.

He crossed the room, still using a black bath sheet to absorb the water beaded across his taut skin. He used one hand to maneuver the towel across the muscles packing his shoulders and eased the other about Dena's trim waist.

"You good?" He gave her a squeeze.

She sighed. "I'd say it's hard to be bad here." She inhaled, soaking in the fresh air approving of its crispness.

"You're shaking," his voice was a low murmur to the top of her head.

"Where'd you learn to do that?" She smiled, still in awe of the fact that he was so in tune to every miniscule glitch in her system.

Soft chuckling shook his expansive torso. "I swear you're the only one I can do it with."

"Well I'm not cold," Dena told him, her voice holding a twinge of surprise over the fact. "Nervous, I guess," she decided feeling a tuft of air near her bare feet. Carlos had let his towel fall.

"You're gonna have to take another shower," She warned.

"What makes you say that?" He faked a bout of confusion.

Dena nudged her bottom against the steady erection that was setting her nerve endings to tingle.

"You should get busy handling that so we won't be late for dinner with Kraven and Darby." Carlos suggested, strong fingers launching a slow massage of her hip.

"It takes a lot to handle you," Dena rested her head against his chest, biting her lip on the sensation he roused when he flexed impressively. "Where do you think I should start?" Her last word softened on a sigh when she felt two, deliciously thick fingers filling her. She convulsed against the unyielding length of him. Her body was only in tune to the surge and rotation of the penetrating caress.

She wanted to turn, but he stifled the move. She was garbed only in the shirt he'd discarded before their nap. She'd planned on joining Carlos in the shower before the balcony called to her. The unbuttoned shirt exposed Dena to the chilly Edinburgh breeze that she'd found more rejuvenating than jolting.

Apparently, Carlos felt the same, unmindful of the cold jostling his bare frame. Tirelessly, he fondled Dena adding his thumb to the act. He stimulated her clit with an affecting graze causing her to squirm wildly next to him.

"Relax…" his voice was a caress; words wrapped in silken tethers and doused with heavy sweetness and depth. "Easy…" he urged, smiling as his tone stoked the desired response within her. His fingers worked her with a fluid, seductive elegance shifting speed and direction.

Dena could only mouth his name; she hadn't the strength to force in sound. The only exertion she desired came in the form of bucking her hips and curving into his devastating assaults. He was weighing a breast, his skillful thumb molesting a pouty nipple.

"Carlos-"

"Shh…take it…" he added more pressure to the massage on her clit and cupped her breast more firmly when she shuddered. "I promise you won't feel so nervous after this…" his thumb was more insistent on the sensitized flesh at the apex of her thighs.

Dena wasn't so sure about not feeling nervous. Not when the man's touch- hell, the man himself; had the power to throw every part of her-nerves included- into a frenzy. She felt him drive his fingers deep, so high the move sent her to her toes and wincing on twin stimulants of pain and pleasure.

His mouth, erotically sculpted and skilled, skimmed her nape and the slope between her neck and shoulder. His thumb and forefinger pinched the nipple that was now a puckered bud erect and pleading for more attention.

"Easy…relax for me…"

"I am…I…mmm…"

"Ah…" His riveting eyes narrowed in satisfaction when he felt her coating his fingers with her moisture.

"That's it," he breathed the words against her shoulder. "That's it," he tongued her ear canal and firmed his hold on her when she trembled violently.

Dena was wilting in the circle of his arms then. She could've sobbed her appreciation when he let her turn. Still taking her with his fingers, he imprisoned her neck in his hand and kissed her with a sensuous savagery.

"Dammit Carlos," Dena hissed when he unexpectedly withdrew from her center. She quickly eased down from her frustration at the realization that he was taking her to bed.

He didn't lay her down, instead he made her stand in front of him on the bed and used the positioning to an impressive advantage. He nurtured himself at her breasts, equally dividing his attention between both nipples until they glistened from merciless bouts of suckling. His nose outlined their shape, tracing the undersides, traveling her ribcage, navel and the bare triangle of skin above her sex.

When Carlos turned his suckling expertise to the responsive patch of flesh that he'd shamelessly aroused beneath his thumb, Dena's legs threatened to give way beneath her. It was no matter, the sweet massage he was then applying to her buttocks served as ample support once she could no longer stand against the intensity of his caresses.

Dena cupped her hands around the back of his head, feeling him bump her palms and thighs each time he shifted direction. A sudden tug, took her off the bed and Dena found herself against a wall her sex being overwhelmed by his a second later.

Carlos claimed her slowly at first, conducting a perfect rhythm that held sync to his resumed feasting on her breasts. The pad of his ring finger tended a nipple and all the while he groaned his pleasure at the sensation of its twin on his tongue. He opened her wider to him, driving his shaft deeper as his lean hips surged with deft purpose.

Dena welcomed the wall at her back and the way Carlos' every thrust sent her head nudging it. He ceased his nibbling on her breasts to settle his forehead in the valley between. He caught her hips, keeping them still to receive the ramming drives that sent the muscles rippling a captivating wave in his toned ass and powerful thighs.

His seed was splashing warm and heavy inside her then. The sensation had an orgasmic effect on Dena and her release mingled with his seconds later. They held one another at the wall for some time. Keeping her secure in his embrace, Carlos took them into the shower.

***

"Mad wench, did she honestly think you'd give her Belle?" Kraven asked.

Dena had just relayed the story of Evangela Leer's visit, the list of demands she'd laid out and Dena's own history with the Leer crew. The couples had reservations at the inn's bistro. They'd requested a remote table where they could chat, away from the direct line of sight of other diners.

"She threatened to tell Carlos that I worked for her and to give him specifics on the things I did during my employment," Dena fidgeted with the edge of her napkin. "I was sure they'd be things he'd never forgive."

Kraven nodded. Relieving Dena of the napkin, he took her hand when she shuddered out the last of her words. If anyone could understand how debilitating it could be to live with the fear of having the past threaten the future with the one you loved, it was him.

"Have you told your family yet?" Darby asked.

147

"You and Kraven are the only family we've told so far."

Darby blinked suddenly, her jade gaze glistening as emotion took hold over Dena's declaration that she and Kraven were indeed family. She squeezed Dena's hand while Kraven lifted the one he held and put a kiss to the back of it.

Carlos studied the threesome. His smile mirrored his contentment. *There she is,* he thought, loving the swing of her bouncy dark locks about her round face and the collar of her gold cashmere sweater. He was as awed by the light he saw in Dena's ebony gaze as he was by what he heard in her laughter. There was the girl he loved, the one he'd glimpsed years later and the one who had returned to be with him always.

"Lord DeBurgh?"

The couples looked up at the waiter who stood smiling down at them.

"The tasting room is ready, Sir." The man said.

Kraven had arranged for him and Carlos to sample from a new line of Scotch by a group of whiskey distillers he'd partnered with. When the guys had ventured off, Dena and Darby put in orders for cheesecake and coffee.

"Congratulations again on the baby," Dena pressed a kiss to Darby's cheek. "I'll be sure to bring an amazing gift when we come back for the shower."

"Well your husband's already a step ahead," Darby scooted her chair closer to the table. "He gave me the most adorable stuffed animal- it's got my expected due month and the year stitched into the tummy. He said he found it at one of the airport shops while you guys were waiting on your flight."

"Did he?" A curious smile held Dena's mouth. "He didn't say a thing."

Darby tugged at the extra-long sleeves of her pearl cowl neck sweater. "Carlos reminds me so much of my Dad that it's scary. Tough guys- both of 'em, they do what has to be done- no questions, no whining, no regrets. Men like them don't always want folks to know what teddy bears they can be."

"That's my husband to a tee," Dena's expression was speculative- doubting. "But I think him not telling me about your gift was about more than that. He's protecting me. The fact that we won't have babies of our own, I guess he didn't want to breech that subject by telling me that he was getting you a gift."

"Damn," Darby closed her eyes, raising a hand to cover her mouth. "Dena I'm sorry."

"Honey why?" Dena tugged at Darby's hand, closing it inside her own. "I'm happy for you guys and I'm happy for Carlos and me. *Finally.* Finally I'm *ecstatic* for us," gleeful tears swam in her dark gaze.

"What do you think our chances were of finding our way back to one another after all the bizarre twists our lives have taken?"

Darby's honey wheat curls; piled high, bounced when she shook her head. "Not good," she said.

"A snowball's chance," Dena added. "I don't plan to waste any more time mourning over what can never be. I want us to celebrate what is."

Darby raised the glass of ginger ale she'd ordered with her dinner, smiling when Dena did the same with her wine. "To a snowball's chance," she cheered.

~~~

"I'll seriously consider kicking your ass if you tell me I can't take a bottle of this back with me."

Kraven's hearty laughter was contagious and quickly traveled to Carlos who had spoken.

"So I guess that means it's up to par?" Kraven asked.

"It's up to par like a muthafucka."

The two fast friends fell into another round of rumbling laughter.

"It's a deal," Kraven helped himself to another hit of the liquor. "I'll have the staff pack a few bottles for you to take back and then I'll ship a few more cases later on." Hand still gripping the bottle, Kraven leveled a finger in Carlos' direction. "You just make sure Fernando doesn't catch a whiff of this. His doctors don't want him on anything but water and juice for the time being."

"Not a problem," Carlos took the bottle of Scotch. "If I run into trouble with him, I'll just tell County."

"Thank God for strong women!" Kraven roared as more laughter rumbled.

"Amen," Carlos thought of his wife. "Did you ever think you'd marry someone as strong as Darby?"

Kraven snorted his laughter then. "I never thought I'd ever *be* married, but no- never. The women I helped myself to asked no questions and their answers ran along the lines of 'yes Kraven', 'anything you say Kraven'."

Carlos nodded, such experiences were ones he could definitely relate to. "You know the time may come when we'll need them to give us just those kinds of answers." He studied the light reflecting off the Scotch. "How far are you willing to go to destroy that island and everybody associated with it?"

"You mean, will I do the things I swore I'd never do again to protect what I love? In a heartbeat," Kraven vowed.

Carlos continued to study his drink. "Even if she begs you not to? Lays down some of that strength to keep you grounded?"

"You don't pose easy questions, friend," Kraven shook his head. "I don't suppose *you've* already thought up an answer to that wee obstacle?"

Carlos chuckled. "Not at all," he tossed back the well-blended Scotch.

"Hmph," Kraven followed suit and emptied his own glass. "Still agree with havin' a strong woman at your side?"

"Wouldn't have it any other way," Carlos took care of their refills.

Shot glasses clinked as soft laughter resumed.

~CHAPTER ELEVEN~

In an effort to keep Casper M'Baye's whereabouts off the grid for as long as possible, Kraven had arranged to have specialists flown into the clinic as opposed to attempting a move to a better equipped hospital. While Casper's condition appeared to be stabilizing, the doctors were still hesitant to confirm that she was totally out of the woods.

The McPheresons and DeBurghs arrived in Near Invernesshire around lunchtime the following afternoon. Around dusk, they were heading into the Mogey Clinic and being greeted by Dr. Leti Bobbin.

"She's stable for the time being, thanks to the very capable staff Lord DeBurgh flew in."

"Now, now Leti…" *Lord DeBurgh* cajoled.

The prim doctor flushed. "I'm sorry, *Kraven.*"

"Dr. Bobbin," Dena took a cautious step forward. "Has she said anything more?"

"The new physicians are keeping her heavily sedated. She's set for another dosing in another hour or so," the doctor smiled understandingly. "She should be a lot more lucid for your chat."

Dena nodded. "Thank you."

"She *is* a bit edgy though," the doctor put a tentative hand on Dena's forearm. "It may still be something of a jolt to have so many visitors."

"I understand Dr. Bobbin, I'm Dena McPhereson and this is my husband Carlos." She sent a smile toward Carlos and then turned back to the doctor. "I'm the one your patient wants to see. The others can wait here if that would be better."

The tiny doctor looked appreciative. "Thank you for understanding, Mrs. McPhereson."

"Could I have a moment? Mrs. McPhereson?" Carlos politely queried, unceremoniously drawing his wife away from the group.

Darby sent the doctor a reassuring smile. "Thank you for your assistance, Dr. Bobbin."

"I'll just check in with the doctor on call," Dr. Bobbin said, not sensing there was anything amiss.

"See?" Kraven chided once the doctor had hurried off. "Carlos isn't going for that 'I'll see the crazy bitch alone' shit, either."

Darby flashed her husband a chilly green glare and then watched the couple debating across the small lobby. She smiled and patted a hand to the middle of Kraven's chest.

"Doesn't look like his wife gives a damn," Darby noted.

Dena was leaving her husband to sulk. "Let's go," she called to Darby.

Darby slipped Kraven a cunning wink and then caught up to Dena. They joined Leti Bobbin down the corridor.

Carlos returned, stopping near Kraven. "Sometimes strong women can be a pain in the ass."

Kraven's rich laughter drew playfully admonishing looks from the nurses.

***

Seattle, Washington~

Quest and Taurus Ramsey looked up in unison when one of the patio doors slid open to reveal a tiny dark girl with a mop of curls and brilliant gray eyes smiling out at them.

"Goodness," Taurus complimented his cousin's two year old. "She can turn a man's brain to mush without saying a word to him."

"I'll take credit for teaching her how to do that," Mick arrived just after her daughter. She went to greet Taurus with a hug while Quincee climbed upon her father's lap to ply him with a noisy kiss.

"Hope we're not runnin' you guys off," Taurus noted, nodding toward the baby bag Mick had placed on the patio table.

"You guys need to talk," Mick pulled at one of the tassels on Taurus' Grambling State sweatshirt. "This'll give me and Quinny some time with Ny."

Quincee had finished giving her dad his morning kisses. She eased down from his lap to carefully waddle around to the opposite side of the square table where she planned to bestow Taurus with the same treatment.

Mick stepped aside, giving Taurus room to stoop and scoop her little girl into his arms. She rubbed a hand over his shoulder before he walked off with Quincee across the patio, engaged in one of the child's endless streams of conversation. That morning's topic centered around the teddy bear stitched on the front of her green corduroy jumper.

"I didn't know you guys were meeting today," Michaela watched the duo for a while before she looked to her husband. "Did we interrupt?"

"We were gonna head in the house for breakfast." Quest stood. "We just met out here on the patio to kick it and what not."

"It'd be great to have Carlos here for this."

"I want more backup than just me and Taurus for that," Quest looked doubtful and commenced to massaging the fraternity brand that ached his upper arm whenever he was stressed. "The man's not gonna take it too well when we tell him this."

Mick watched Taurus pointing out across the patio toward something Quincee had discovered. "What about Pike? Have you thought about how best to handle things with him and Belle?"

Groaning then, Quest settled to the edge of the glass patio table and folded his arms over his chest. "Another big conversation to hold with a big crowd," He reached for the edge of Mick's sweatshirt and pulled her to him.

155

"This could ruin Jasper Stone's relationship with Carmen as well as his new one with Belle." Quest's left dimpled grin emerged though ruefully. "Why are we always the lucky ones to get the newest info first?"

"Good things come to those who wait?" Mick sighed and then scrunched her small nose. "Don't think that applies here, huh?"

"I love you," Quest murmured into her neck as they hugged.

***

Had the woman lying in the slim elevated bed passed her on the street, Dena doubted she'd have recognized her. Darby's picture had in fact done more to trigger her memory than the actual sight of Casper M'Baye lying beneath the mountain of blankets. Her slight flinching beneath the covers, told Dena that she may've been on the verge of waking.

Casper M'Baye opened her eyes and spent several seconds blinking as she labored to focus on her surroundings.

"Cas?"

Even the soft call of her name was enough to send Casper jerking as though she were attempting to shrink deeper into the covers.

"Casper, it's me Dena. Dena Ramsey," Dena made no attempts to move any closer to the bed. "Casper do you remember asking for me?"

The 'deer caught in headlights' look slowly faded from Casper's dark eyes to make room for a trace of recognition. "Dena?"

Dena confirmed with a single nod.

"Dena? Dena you-you have to get out. Find someplace to-" She pushed free of the covers extending both hands to her former associate. "You have to get someplace safer. They're coming, they..." Casper proceeded to recap the panicked warnings she'd spouted to anyone who would listen over the last several days.

"...they found you. They- Saffron and those fucking computers of hers- tracked you down. Eva," she took a moment to swallow and bring relief to her dry throat. "Eva was pissed to find out you were married and happy after just walking out like that..." Casper's hands clenched and unclenched over the sleeves of Dena's sweater.

"Be careful, Denny- they're coming after you. They want you to clear a way to get them to your cousin Belle. Eva wants to use her to draw out Captain Perjas. She found out he's your cousin's father- saw a wedding photo online- courtesy of Saf. I know this sounds crazy, but you have to believe me!"

"I do, Cas. I do," Dena spoke in soothing tones thinking it wise to get Casper to calm down a bit. "Honey shh...shh...it's alright. Eva and Mae found me and it's alright."

Casper went completely still and; for a moment, Dena thought she'd gone into shock.

"Are they dead?"

"No," Dena shook her head unable to tell if it was relief or disappointment she saw fill the woman's haunted stare.

"You were smart to leave, Dena," Eerie flatness had taken hold of Casper's voice. "You were so smart."

"No. I was just too afraid to stay." Dena moved to the chair near Casper's bed. "I was afraid of myself- of what I was turning into."

"Hmph," Casper appeared to relax a little settling into the covers. "We're a pair, Den. *You* left because you were afraid of yourself. I *stayed* because I was afraid of Eva."

Casper began to cough then and Dena fetched water. She took a seat on the edge of the bed and helped the woman to swallow a bit.

"Why did you come here, D?" Casper asked once she'd taken her fill of the water. "You have to know how I wound up in here. Why didn't you tell them to tell me to go fuck myself when they said I wanted to see you?"

"I was curious," Dena set the water cup to the bedside table. "I wanted to know what you had to tell me."

Casper smiled miserably. "Guess it was a trip hearing me snitch on Eva, huh?"

"Maybe you're finally becoming more afraid of what you're turning into than you are of Eva."

Casper hissed through her teeth. "I'm not *turning into* anything Dena. I'm already turned and there's no going back." She caught at the sheets, gave them a tug.

"This is probably the bed I'll die in. Guess I'm just trying to clear my conscience before I face my judgment. That's a laugh, right?"

You said Eva and Mae found you but...they aren't dead? How is that possible?" She shifted her head on the pillows. "Are they being held?"

"They let me go so I could help them."

"I can't believe that she actually thought you'd give over your own cousin." Casper worked her fingers against the bridge of her nose.

"In her defense, she was just playing the odds. The 'Denny' Evangela knew was a weak, guilt ridden little girl desperate to redeem herself in the eyes of those she'd wronged..." Dena smirked over her word choice.

"You didn't *wrong* anybody," Casper argued.

"Well," Dena gave a resolving smile. "I was working with enough guilt to convince myself that I had. It's played me until this very day. Eva figured she had me- all the crap she was holding over my head... everything she knew she threatened to tell my husband." She raised a brow toward Casper. "What woman would want her husband to know such things?"

"What happened?" Casper was riveted on the story.

Dena smiled. "To understand that, you have to know the kind of man my husband is. Suffice it to say, he loves me regardless. I've got something as close to unconditional love as anyone can get, Cas. I told him my secrets and he told me he loves me."

"Were your husband another kind of man, Eva may've won out playing her odds." Casper sniffled when sudden emotion claimed its hold.

"No," Dena was adamant then. "I would've never given that bitch my cousin."

Casper evidently believed what she saw in Dena's eyes. "What were you saying about being weak?" She gave a resolute nod. "What little strength I *thought* I had would pose a pretty pitiful opponent against everything E holds over *my* head."

"Yeah," Dena settled against the bedside chair. "The woman *does* love her info, doesn't she?" Dena waited for Casper to look her way. "Did she ever say anything about a research facility? She mentioned something to me. It's a place not part of the island. She thinks the Captain may know where it is."

"Not on the island?" Casper frowned.

"Sounded like she was referring to a whole other locale."

"No Dena," Casper still frowned appearing bewildered as well as suspicious. "She never told me about a place like that," she squeezed her eyes shut as if pained. "Hell, maybe she did and my brain's still too mushy to recall. Maybe she did say something...she told me so much." She studied Dena for a full minute. "We got really close-especially after you left. God...the stuff she told me-all the way back to when she first got hooked up in all this."

"I guess people like her need a friend, a confidant. She sure couldn't have girl to girl chats with Mae. Hmph, we'd laugh so much over the fools in charge- like those clowns Cufi and Yvonne." She seemed to sadden.

"It helped to find humor in them, in the whole damn thing. That place in Nice...any one of us could've probably walked right out of there and they wouldn't have noticed 'til we were halfway to Britain."

Something bittersweet clouded her wide expressive eyes as she thought of her 'captors'. "Those two... they spent more time arguing than anything else. Drove Eva batshit. Me? Hmph, reminded me of my dear old mom and step dad. So many spats, so many..."

~~~

"More coffee guys?" Darby's tone was chipper as she watched the two stormy-eyed giants who shared her table.

"Givin' her five more minutes in there with that lunatic," Carlos muttered.

"Second," Kraven agreed, giving a confrontational shrug when Darby pinned him with a look.

They had decided-or rather- Darby had decided they'd be more comfortable waiting in the clinic's cafeteria. The food was marvelous, the coffee spectacular and the threesome just managed to keep their minds off what was going on between Dena and her old acquaintance.

The guys however, were losing patience. Darby could see that in the way they kept checking their watches and the wall clocks. When Carlos made an impressive show of cracking all ten of his knuckles with a simultaneous clench of two fists, Darby knew Dena's trip down memory lane was about to be interrupted.

"You guys are worrying too much," Darby leaned forward, spreading her hands out across the table. "Dena's proven she can handle herself. She *was* an assassin after all."

"She hasn't been that in a long time," Carlos muttered.

"True," Darby proceeded cautiously, "but didn't you tell us she managed to put you on your ass and disarm you in your own home?"

Carlos downed the rest of the coffee that had grown tepid in his mug and sent Kraven a look. "Tell your wife I'm thinking about taking back my baby gift." He said.

Laughter chorused among the small group, making way for tension to escape. When there was quiet between them, Darby reached out to take Carlos' loose fist between her hands. She smiled when he unclenched his fingers and laced them between hers.

"And look whose here," Darby sighed, drawing the men's attention toward Dena crossing the cozy cafeteria.

Carlos went to Dena, stopping her trip across the dining area when he moved before her. He merely cupped her face, searching her eyes as though he only needed to do so in order to decide if she was alright.

Dena squeezed his hands. Taking one, she led him back to the table and pushed him down into the chair he'd relinquished.

"Sorry I took so long. I got the doctors to extend our time," Dena pushed her hair back from her face, refusing the chair Darby offered. "Casper drifted off without being sedated. The doctors say she should wake up in another hour or so. I'd like to stick around…see if she has more to say."

"Did she tell you anything worth hearing?" Darby punched Kraven's thigh when he snorted at her question.

"Oh yeah," Dena's nod was slow, steady. "She did. I'll um-we'll have to discuss it on the way to the airport. We need the earliest flight out."

Darby scooted her chair closer to the table. "What is it? Who are they coming after?"

162

"It's not like that I-it's..." Clearly Dena was too disconcerted to be more descriptive.

"Let's get the hell out of here," Carlos captured Dena's wrist and tugged.

Dena smoothed her hand across his. "I want to see her one more time, baby and then- then we need to go home."

***

Three Hours Later...

"It's a load of bollocks, I tell you."

"Kraven's right, Dena. It *is* pretty coincidental. Not to mention outrageous."

"And convenient," Kraven added.

"I believe it," Dena waved off the server's offer to top off her coffee.

Following the revealing discussion with Casper M'Baye, the McPheresons and the DeBurghs stopped off at the Baird Pub. Coffee was the extent of their order, the group feeling the need for caffeine's kick following the story Dena had just shared.

"This group is as clever as they are psychotic, Dena. You know that better than anybody." Darby offered up her cup for another hit of the French roast. "Maybe this was all part of some contingency plan. If one of 'em got caught, put on this wild act to get you here and then run down this mad story."

Dena propped her elbows before her on the round mahogany table they all shared. "You guys are right, I just…" She drew all ten fingers back through her hair and gave it a tug.

"Hey?" The smooth depth of Carlos' voice eased in then. "You just what?"

Dena smiled when he pulled one hand from her hair and smothered it inside both of his. "I'm a fool to believe a word from anyone associated with that bunch, but it's just outlandish enough to have merit."

Carlos studied his ring on her finger. Slowly, he dragged his thumb across the etching of their names joined around the band. "You've got me, Babe. Whatever you want to do, I have your back."

Dena's smile trembled, yet it remained. "I um…I should talk to the family first. At least to two of the most calm… even tempered…"

Silence held at the table only a few seconds-if that. Kraven's sudden snort was followed by Carlos' deep chuckle which ushered in a wave of necessary laughter among the foursome.

"Calm," Kraven blurted. "Among *this* lot?"

"*And* even tempered," Carlos added, attempting to massage the smirk from his mouth.

"The two I have in mind are calm and even tempered…enough," Dena rested her head against the high back of the majestic armchair she occupied at the table. Closing her eyes, she prayed she was right.

~CHAPTER TWELVE~

Seattle, Washington~

Dena burst into her home like a cyclonic wind had powered her through the front door. "Glad those bitches didn't trash the house!" She called, dropping her purse and overnight bag to the foyer's hardwood flooring. "The house is a good place to talk, right? Or should we go out?"

Carlos deposited the rest of the luggage near where Dena had set her things. He kicked the front door shut while slipping a tan suede jacket from his shoulders. He moved into the house at a much calmer, slower pace than his wife. Tossing aside the quarter length garment, he caught Dena easily before she could take the stairs up to the next level.

"The house is fine," he murmured into her temple, "but I need you to breathe, need you to cool down."

"I have to call-"

"I know babe, shh…"

"You promised-"

"I know babe, I didn't forget, but I need you to calm down. Will you do that for me?"

The request brought on a rush of weariness, turning Dena's legs to water. Carlos simply firmed his hold, keeping her securely sealed against him. "We're going to bed," he announced.

"But the call-"

"We'll call, I promised, didn't I?"

"But do you agree that we should?" Dena gauged his reaction, watching him closely even as he led her up the carpeted staircase.

"I agree," he seemed puzzled. "Did you think I wouldn't?"

She lifted her brows in a show of resignation. "Things like this are usually discussed among a few and then hidden for the well being of all."

"There's been enough of that, don't you think?"

"I do. Do you think they will?"

"We'll find out tomorrow."

"Tomorrow? But I thought- tonight-"

"Tonight," Carlos swung Dena up high against him, deciding to carry her the rest of the way. "Tonight I want to sleep with my wife in our bed. Our *own* bed."

"That's free of secrets," she cupped his jaw and leaned in for the kiss he offered.

In their room, Carlos set Dena to the bed's edge and stripped her to her panties. She kept her eyes on his disturbingly attractive face, loving the attempt he made at trying to remain unaffected, un-aroused while focusing on putting her down to rest.

"Mmm mmm," he resisted her help when she reached out to undo the buttons on the black cotton shirt he wore. He didn't look her way while tucking her beneath the covers.

"You need sleep before tackling all this."

"I need more than sleep," she propped up on an elbow and challenged him. "Are you at least coming to bed?"

Carlos dropped a kiss to her forehead, then tipped her chin up and put one on her mouth. "Nothing's keeping me out of here tonight." He straightened, headed for the door. "Just some things I need to do around the house first."

Tension strained the baby doll softness of her face. "Do you think they'll come back?"

"I almost hope they will," pure wickedness glinted in his striking pale greens. "It'll finally give the security system the workout it deserves." He sent her a wink. "I love you, always will."

"I love you, always have," she blew him a kiss.

~~~

Sleep visited Dena quickly, Carlos returned to the bedroom an hour later to find his wife in a restful doze. It didn't take long to reset the security system levels and catch up on a bit of work he'd missed over the last few weeks. He'd even unpacked the luggage and did a few loads of laundry before he decided to call it a night.

He hoped Dena was sleeping deeply enough so as not to be disturbed by his presence in bed. Deep enough, so he'd feel like too much of a heel for disturbing her.

Disturbance of anything aside from the covers was all Carlos realized he was up to. Once unclothed and burrowed beneath the sheets, he drifted off as soundly as his wife.

~~~

Carlos thought he was dreaming when he woke much later to the feel of her mouth skimming his chest. Hands spanning her waist, Carlos tugged when his fingers curved into the seat of her panties.

"I'm sure you haven't been out long enough," he said, feeling her easing upward to lay prone against him.

"I'm hoping you can put me back to sleep," she murmured, mouth gliding over the vein that flexed at his throat.

"What do you suggest I use?" He felt her mouth curve into a smile and predicted her answer. He felt the scrape of lace next to his bare dick and closed his eyes on the sensation.

Dena tortured him with slow grinding, rubbing his erection and shivering in triumph. "Still need persuasion?" She taunted. A low rumble akin to a growl vibrated against her mouth when her lips trekked his sternum.

Carlos rested a forearm across his eyes relishing the slow caress of her thick hair moving in a downward glide along his torso as she ventured closer to his sex. He couldn't resist cradling her head; holding her gently between his palms when she tongued his naval. He wanted the sensual path she'd charted to reach its intended destination.

Dena obliged, using her nose to outline the trail that included a journey across the muscular range of his thigh, the unyielding length of a thoroughly rigid shaft. When she took him into her mouth, his broad frame bucked.

Carlos' hands weakened, sliding to his sides where he seized the tangled covers and made slight thrusting moves where she pleasured him. Her soft moaning as she suckled and intimately bathed him progressively drained him of all but his lust for her.

She mastered his body's every reaction and he wanted to see her. Somehow, he willed his hand toward a bedside lamp, fiddling with it until the room was illuminated in a soft golden hue.

Then, he absorbed the vision she cast. He was captivated by the bounce and swing of her hair as she loved him with her mouth. She added some twist to the oral attention she shared, causing Carlos to work his head deeper into the pillow cradling it. A familiar tightening fanned out, sending a savory burning to his groin- a demand for release.

"I need to come, D," his voice was thick, rougher sounding with the desire claiming it.

"So do it," she coaxed in the midst of treating him.

"Not ready…not ready," he winced suspended between need and want.

Dena didn't appear to be in the mood to offer pity. She resumed her whimpering moans as her lips and tongue tirelessly swept his length.

Carlos took a fistful of her hair, disengaging her and; in the process, fighting off the fanning flames of arousal that promised culmination sooner than he would have desired it.

Dena smoothly wrenched her hair from his weak grasp. She straddled him, studying his gorgeous features-the face flushing a rich burgundy. The innocence overriding her dark gaze belied something wicked-intensified when she wiped his moisture from the curve of her plump mouth.

Carlos winced something obscene and Dena followed suit; gasping at the sound of her panties ripping beneath the deft jerk he gave them. Big hands smothered her waist, only to lift and settle her beautifully. Dena's inhale was a sharp cry and she bit her lip when he filled her.

He exchanged his grip on her waist for one at her wrists. He kept them immobile at her sides when all Dena wanted was to drag her nails across his artfully crafted torso.

Something incoherent drifted past her parted lips while she rode him slow; interchanging languid up and down moves with indulgent rotations, as she clenched her intimate walls about him and delighted in the vibrant throbs he favored her with in return. Carlos relinquished his hold on her wrists. He was beckoned then by the healthy bounce of her breasts as she so eagerly labored above him. He smoothed a hand inside the silken valley existing between the beautiful licorice orbs before cupping one. He assaulted her areola, bathing the area beneath his thumb until the nipple pouted for the same treatment.

Dena's breaths turned raspy, disjointed as climax neared. Sensing the orgasm about to spasm through her, Carlos put her on her back in the space of a second.

His mouth was everywhere, hot and hungry. His tongue, stroked and suckled, his teeth grazed- marking her as his. Of course that fact had; and would never be challenged. Dena arched, insane to have him inside her again. She hissed a gasp when he put her to her stomach and took her from behind. The moan she felt pressuring her larynx was stifled by the sensations abounding. A hand curved over her hip, thumb and forefinger conspiring in a rueful double-team on her labia.

An array of sensation stemmed from his sex; spreading and exploring hers, while his fingers fondled the fleshy, hypersensitive mound of her clit. Those fingers delved inside her femininity to partner with his dick and Dena wanted to melt into the covers. She was at his mercy after all and savored taking what he so vigorously gave. Orgasm had its way with her as potently as her husband did. Dena felt the heavy downpour of satisfaction steadily coursing to coat his fingers, shaft and the sheets beneath her body.

The effect on Carlos was equally climactic. He gave into the sensational rigors of satisfaction a short time later. Still intimately connected; he covered Dena- her body beneath his, and toiled to slow his breathing.

When he would have rolled off to give her relief from his weight, she hooked her hand around as much of his thigh as she could. "Mmm mmm," she grunted, eyes closed and languishing in total contentment.

Carlos only chuckled and relaxed into her. Sleep revisited quickly and deeply.

***

"How's it hangin', man? Or should I ask one of your former roomies?"

Bashir Cannon's grin was broad across his dark face when he entered the grim, fluorescent lit area. "You need some new material man. I been out seven years," he remarked of the prison stint he'd accepted to secure his cover.

Dreck Eamon returned his partner's grin, drawing the man close for a handshake and hug. "Sorry kid, that shit's never gonna get old."

"Til it's *your* turn." Bashir forewarned.

"Screw that, I'm too pretty for the pen." Dreck smoothed the back of his hand across his jaw.

Bashir waved off his old friend and turned to the man who had accompanied him. "Tesano," he greeted with a nod and extended hand.

Caiphus leaned in for the shake. "Good to see you, Bash. Congratulations. Three years overdue, but better late than never."

Nodding, Bashir accepted the jibe. His prison stint and the connections made during his time there had earned him a prime spot within the Tesano family organization.

"Anything you can tell us from your end?" Caiphus reclaimed the metal chair he'd occupied in the underground chamber where he and Dreck had waited.

"Lots," Bashir said though his expression was discouraging. "Nothing you're interested in hearing about though."

"Fuck," Caiphus slammed a fist to the folding table his chair flanked. His sapphire gaze was dark with emotion. "What about my uncle? Is he close to anybody that you've been able to tell?"

"Besides his brother?"

"Gabriel."

Bashir nodded, scrolling through his phone then. "Hard to say. He doesn't stay in one place very long."

Caiphus tilted his head a fraction. "How long?"

"Stays put two, sometimes three weeks and then jets off again- different place every time," Bashir pulled his own metal chair closer to the table then. "Once a month, he has a chat with this guy," he turned his mobile toward Caiphus and Dreck.

"Who is he?" Dreck asked.

"Haven't ID'd him yet. Haven't found anybody who can."

"Keep at it," Caiphus frowned at the image on the faceplate a second longer before pushing the mobile across the table. "Not too diligently, though."

Bashir pocketed the phone. "Understood."

***

"Why didn't you tell me, Honey?" The devastation in Taurus Ramsey's extraordinary champagne stare was proportionate to the pain in his rich voice.

Dena left Carlos' side to join her brother. "Sweetie, I couldn't," she kissed Taurus' cheek and dragged her fingers through the thick mass of silky light brown covering his head. "Just thinking about Carlos knowing was paralyzing enough." She took his hands then and squeezed.

"I know you always thought you were the butt of some sick joke having Mama and Daddy for parents." She sighed resolvedly. "I couldn't have you knowing what I was and realizing I was even more screwed up than they were."

"You were a scared kid. We were all scared kids." Quest's quietly stirring voice merged into the conversation.

Dena bowed her head, reaching back to squeeze the hand he put to her shoulder. "You and Quay would've been running Ramsey years before you started, if it weren't for what my dad did-"

"D-"

"No Quest," she shook her head once, the gesture tolerating no argument from her cousin. "What happened to Sera- what it stirred up, especially for Quay." Dena thought back to the thunderstorm of scrutiny Quaysar Ramsey had suffered following Sera Black's murder before the Ramsey name and influence had made it all go away. Quest refused to start college until his twin could follow. "You guys almost wound up graduating with Sabra for goodness sake!" She smiled.

"It would've never been that bad," Quest pretended to shudder over the thought while drawing his cousin into a hug.

174

Carlos and Dena had decided that Taurus and Quest would be first on the list to connect with following the Scotland trip. They had arranged to meet for drinks the following evening at Carlos' and Dena's place.

"Will you at least let me apologize for having your guy in Switzerland waste all that time trying to track down Daddy's leaking money?"

Dena had explained to Quest and Taurus the hows and whys of her involvement with Evangela Leer and her associates.

Quest smiled at her reference to Drake Reinard a good friend and the CFO of Ramsey's European offices. "I wish you would've come to us. Any of us." He scolded lightly while kissing the back of her hand. "But I understand why you didn't."

"You do?" Her dark eyes flashed with expectancy.

"Every family has secrets," Quest's hazy gray eyes succumbed to the inky blackness they adopted when temper was upon him. "The ones in our family go beyond those of the average group." He shrugged beneath the gun-metal gray hoody he sported.

"As long as I can remember, the issues in our family have been so insanely insurmountable that it's easier just to bury them." He dropped another kiss to her hand and released it.

"When it comes to the shit in our own personal lives, it seems the 'bury it' procedure is the way to go- it's all we know. I don't think any of us are in a position to judge you for doing what you thought you had to do."

"Doing what you think you have to do is exhausting," Dena confessed. "It's a burden no one should

175

always have to bear on their own." She scooted closer to kiss Quest's cheek and then Taurus' before returning to the loveseat she'd shared with Carlos.

"I don't want to live like that anymore." She told her brother and cousin. "I don't want to bear the weight of...*things* on my own anymore and especially not when I believe it's family business."

Taurus' stare faltered a fraction and he traded a look with Quest. A moment later, both men looked to Carlos for clarification.

Carlos had been sitting quietly at Dena's side and he continued to do so. He merely rubbed a hand across his wife's back in a show of encouragement.

Fortified by what she needed to continue, Dena leaned forward crossing her legs beneath the powder blue lounge dress she'd selected for the intimate chat.

"There's more and it isn't something meant to be kept among a few." She hesitated then for effect and not out of unease. "What we need to discuss now is how best to share it."

~CHAPTER THIRTEEN~

It was decided that Carlos and Dena would open their home again the next evening. That night's event: a late family supper. Dena had been riding a wave of nervous energy since the previous night and decided to put it all to good use and prepare the entire supper herself. She worked in the kitchen for the better part of the day.

Guests arrived at the McPhereson's to a meal of succulent roast turkey breasts, smothered in red and green onions, chives and cherry tomatoes. White rice with a hearty turkey gravy, steamed broccoli and cauliflower along with a fruit tart for dessert completed the filling meal.

In spite of the subject about to be discussed, the evening began in an easy enough fashion. The food roused lots of compliments. The majority of the dinner table conversation surrounded the recent pre-holiday couples getaway. Once dessert was polished off, no one seemed in a mood to leave the table. The group opted to enjoy coffee and drinks right there.

Carlos took Dena by the hand, gave a warning squeeze to let her know it was time.

"You okay?" He asked beneath the veil of soft conversation between their other guests.

Understandably hesitant, Dena barely managed a nod. "I don't want to do more harm than good. We don't even know it- maybe it's all for the best that I-"

"Hey? Ask yourself this- knowing her as well as you do, do you think she'd appreciate being once again kept in the dark for her own good? Or would she want every scrap of info she could get her hands on?"

The questions battled Dena's hesitation and won. With a minute nod, she turned toward her four guests. She gave Taurus and Quest a look before calling out to their wives.

"Nile? Mick? How 'bout we take our coffee to the sitting room?"

~~~

"Sabra was the most…vocal about it, but we were all pretty worried," Michaela was saying once she, Nile and Dena were enjoying large mugs of a delicious hazelnut roast from a new pot.

"I *am* sorry for worrying you guys," Dena's gaze shifted between her two guests. "Quest and T told you how I um…know Evangela Leer?" She reciprocated the nod

Mick and Nile gave. "Please believe that I never meant to deceive any of you. I know that sounds weak considering how long we've all known each other-" She stopped when Nile reached over to squeeze her hand.

"The person you were helped make you the person you are and we all love you." Nile said.

"Honey did you think our feelings would change because of this? Is that why you wanted to talk privately?" Mick asked.

Dena regarded the sitting room that was really a cozy alcove just off from the dining room. The area was furnished with a set consisting of a cushiony mocha brown sofa, two flanking chairs and a coffeetable. The floor lamps beamed dim gold light so as not to completely obstruct the view beyond the windows overlooking the rear lawn.

"Actually there's more to it, Mick and I thought it'd be better to tell you myself." She took a deep, steadying breath. "One of Eva's people suffered serious injuries after the dog attack at Kraven's and Darby's. She managed to make it off the property but the extent of her injuries landed her at a clinic not far from the estate."

"Poor thing," Michaela made no apologies for her sarcasm.

Dena smiled. "The clinic-covering their bases, tried to find out who she was. They called Kraven considering the proximity. She started raving- they believed it was a direct result of her injuries. They still don't know if she'll survive this. During her ravings, she called out for me- said she had to warn me. I figured it was about the visit from Mae and Eva and it was…pretty much…we started talking about the old days and how much she admired me for getting out of it. She told me what happened with her relationship to Eva once I was gone."

Nile looked to Michaela who shrugged.

"Loyalty was real big with Evangela," Dena continued, "when I left, she spent a lot of time licking her wounds, a lot of time cursing me-Casper was there to lend an ear."

"Casper?" Mick queried.

"Casper M'Baye, Eva's confidant."

"Hmph, I thought that'd be the other one, Maeva," Nile considered.

"No, Hon," Dena graced her sister-in-law with a prophetic smile. "Maeva Leer is psychotic, a mental handicap. I don't know if Evangela would admit that to anyone except maybe herself. Casper was always Eva's confidant, her go to person until I came along. The fact that we were supposedly blood, put Cas in the back seat then."

"I still can't believe that," Nile drew fingers through her straight dark hair while shaking her head.

"I didn't even know it at the time, but looking back-the way she took to me...makes sense," Dena said.

"Damn right it makes sense," Mick's mouth was curved into a distasteful sneer. "Marc was bound to have another bat-shit crazy kid lurking about."

Quiet settled before a burst of conjoined laughter eased some of the heaviness.

"During our chat, Casper went on about her relationship with Evangela- all the things they'd shared."

Mick snorted then. "Guess we know where *her* loyalties lie."

"For all Eva's faults, she does have an…ability to draw a person in- to make them feel safe, make them feel their well-being is her top priority and that she'd never betray that." Dena explained. "Confiding in Casper only solidified those feelings."

"So in other words, we shouldn't count on Miss M'Baye to help us learn anything more about the island or this research park Eva wants you to help her find?" Mick asked.

"It's hard to say," Dena settled back on the sofa, folding her arms across the off-shoulder Tee she wore with lavender yoga pants. "Casper claims she never heard of the place Eva mentioned. We mostly discussed old conversations that took place between her and Eva- mostly ones Evangela overheard between your parents," she looked to Nile.

"Cufi and Yvonne?" Nile rephrased, taken aback.

Dena responded with a slow nod. "You see, Eva was there almost from the jump- there on the island and then she moved between other locations wherever she was needed."

"But that's insane. I mean, was she an employee or a victim?" Nile was incredulous.

"Hard to tell," Dena shrugged, "according to Casper, she was a runaway like her. Casper was sleeping under a shed at the L.A. docks waiting on some fantasy ship she'd heard about at one of the teen homeless shelters she frequented as a kid. She thought she'd found her salvation when The Wind Rage arrived to take her to parts unknown. That's how she met Eva."

181

"The Wind Rage," Mick whispered the name of the fated ship.

"She did say that Evangela *seemed* to get the same treatment as the rest of them. The young women quickly discovered that the island, the ship and the mansion in Nice weren't their tickets to leisure, but *work*- of a most intimate sort."

Nile bowed her head, feeling sudden cold kissing her skin through the sleeves of her caramel cashmere sweater. Silently, she recalled the various *duties* given to the young women in her father's employ.

"Casper said she remembers there were times when Eva seemed like she was in charge." Dena said.

"Like a madam," Mick guessed.

Dena nodded. "Madam, mentor, nanny..."

It was Mick's turn to fall silent. She recalled that many of the girls taken were of an age where such chaperones would be required.

"Those responsibilities were left to Evangela to be delegated. Basically, she got the place running properly, visited for...maintenance checks of a sort and then it was back to the island. She was there when your mother arrived." Dena spoke to Mick, referencing Evette Sellars who had changed her name to Yvonne Wilson after she married Cufi Muhammad. "We all know that she became almost as powerful as her husband before the end but when she *first* arrived she was very young and very much out of her element- all that combined with the fact that she had to leave her only child."

Michaela bristled, her amber stare narrowing in on Dena's face. "That's probably the one thing she never stressed over."

"According to Casper via Evangela, there was a fair amount of stress. Apparently, they argued all the time about her leaving you. It got so bad, that Cufi brought his own daughter to live with them." Dena looked to Nile whose dark eyes were wide with expectancy.

Mick was blinking profusely, her trick to stifle tears. "What are you trying to say Dena? That she was all of a sudden so torn up over leaving me, that Cufi Muhammad was benevolent enough to give her a new little girl to raise?"

Dena's blinking didn't work as well at battling tears. She used the sleeve of her shirt to wipe at a trickle of moisture. "According to Casper, Yvonne didn't leave you because she wanted to. She left you because she had to-"

"Bullshit," Mick hissed, hands shaking so badly, that she set her mug to the low coffee table between her chair and the sofa that Dena and Nile occupied. "She's fucking with you Dena. For whatever reason, Casper M'Baye's filling your head with a load of nonsense!" She clenched fists to her jean clad thighs.

"That may be true Mick, but what reason would she have?" Dena scooted to the sofa's edge. "Honey Yvonne's dead and Casper believes she soon will be. This was only a small part of what we discussed- the most lucid part. When I suspected it was *you* she was talking about, I urged her to keep going on that line of the conversation."

"So did the bitch clue you in on just why Yvonne thought she *had* to leave me?" Mick snapped.

"You remember Cufi's specialty?" Dena looked to her fingers fidgeting with them. "It was something he'd dabbled in long before he changed his name from Charlton Browning which is who he was when he met your mother. Prostitution was a big part of his game…and hers."

Michaela seemed to wilt and silence flooded the tiny space for a time.

"Finish it, Dena," Mick's voice was flat, practically monotone. "This is all leading somewhere, isn't it?"

"Yvonne seemed okay with what she'd done and then she started giving Cufi grief over it- people started talking." Dena tugged at the loose ponytail she'd fashioned. "Yvonne didn't care when she flew off the handle about you. She let it go for a while when Cufi told her you'd be expected to…earn your stay same as all the rest. Then he brought Nile to smooth things over. He lost some of his hard-heartedness then. He loved Nile-adored her. Treasured her as his daughter. She was his blood and he'd never think of involving her in something like that. He softened after a while, tried to find you, but you were already caught up in the system. He couldn't risk snooping too deeply and having anything being traced back to him. Casper says it was around that time that he changed his name."

"Jesu, how does this woman know these things?" Nile was still in a state of disbelief.

Dena smiled understandingly. "Information accounts for the bulk of Evangela Leer's wealth. Between the ship, the place in Nice and the island, she accrued scores of it and used it-made unspeakable amounts of money off it. Yvonne and Cufi were two of the earliest and…easiest to glean information from."

"Why did they look for me?" Michaela's voice was unnervingly hollow when it filtered in that time. "What made him change his mind after all that time? His love for Nile?"

"Casper said, according to Evangela that Cufi's 'everybody earns their stay' decree didn't pertain to Yvonne or Nile. He didn't have Nile living with him before, mainly because he didn't want her involved in the nasty side of his business. Despite the monster he was, it appeared that he loved her. Her living there, seeing her everyday it must've triggered something. Not even Evangela knows for sure. But when Yvonne reminded him that he had another daughter-"

"No," Mick's voice regained strength. She moved to the edge of her chair, ready to stand.

Dena moved to sit on the coffee table. "She says he tried to find you, but doing that meant putting himself at risk of being found. He told Yvonne to forget it, reminding *her* that she was as much a criminal as he was so they- they let you go."

Michaela was shaking her head. The tears she'd stifled were then loosed and streaming her dark lovely face. On weakened fists, she pushed herself from the chair.

"Mick!" Nile stood as well, calling out to the woman she had long since claimed as her sister.

Stumbling on the blocky heels of her low cut boots, Mick made her way to the alcove's open entryway. Momentarily, she braced on the doorframe for support and then pushed off.

"Mick!" Dena called, "Wait!" She rushed out along with Nile.

Carlos, Taurus and Quest had remained in the dining room. They attempted conversation but were mostly eavesdropping on the discussion between their wives. When Michaela burst out of the alcove, Quest was already there to grab her and hold tight.

Michaela let her husband apply the soothing rubs between her shoulder blades that always fixed whatever ailed her. Her breathing slowed yet gradually resumed its churning speed. She wrenched out of his embrace to continue her stumbling trek towards the front door.

"Mick-!"

"Quest wait!" Nile extended her hands as she ran after Michaela.

Amidst the commotion, Carlos only saw Dena still in the alcove doorway. Twisting her hands, she looked as lost as she'd been on the night she began to tell him her secrets. With his pale stare solely fixed on her, Carlos crossed to Dena and drew her against him.

He only held her rigid form in his arms; moving his palms up and down her back, her hips and up again. He applied the slightest pressure to the nape of her neck, until he felt her grow pliant next to him. He rocked her when she shuddered beneath an onslaught of sobs that worked their way into her throat and demanded release.

"That's it, that's it..." Carlos cheered his approval of the full, draining cries that shook her body.

Taurus left Quest's side then. He joined Carlos and Dena, dipping his head to press a kiss to his sister's temple before linking his arms about she and Carlos while emotion had its way.

"Is it true? Do you think it's true?" Mick asked Nile.

They stood out in the driveway seemingly unaware of the brisk wind lifting their hair and ruffling their sweaters.

"I'm sure it is," Nile paced a little circle near Mick. "There're tests though that we can take to determine if there is a DNA match in our blood or something I suppose..." she stopped her pacing, turned to Michaela. "I don't need any of that to tell me you're my sister."

"Thanks Nile," Mick's smile was genuine.

Nile however, was frowning. "That wasn't a sentimental statement. It's fact. I used to ask Maman-Yvonne why she loved me. She...she wasn't my mother. My real mother was dead, that much I understood in spite of my age. But Yvonne did love me; that much I also knew so the question became like our little thing." Nile turned her face into the chilly breeze letting it rejuvenate her.

"I'd ask 'Why do you love me?' and she'd say she loved me because I was Daddy's girl and Daddy had given her sweet girls. I always thought she was talking about the other girls at the mansion."

"Maybe she was," Mick continued to stare off towards the wooded expanse across the street. "If all this...craziness is true, why didn't they try to find me later when I'd grown up? They wouldn't have had to worry about the system then."

"Michaela," The incredulous tone returned to Nile's voice. "Are you hearing yourself? Do you really think they could've wooed you into that lifestyle in your early twenties? Still too risky and my situation was little better. The older I got, the more of a problem I had with my father's business. In time, he saw that as a threat. All that love Mademoiselle Leer thinks he had for me took a backseat to the protection of his business. I got left behind in the States too, remember?"

"Yeah…with family. She loved you enough to care." Mick's voice was small.

Nile moved closer. "Maybe she cared because she never forgot what she left you to suffer through back here."

"Don't," Mick turned and put a bit more space between herself and Nile. "Don't make me pity her."

"I wouldn't do that, Michaela but all your life you've thought you were unloved." Nile shook her head decisively. "I can't imagine anyone not wanting to discover that there was a chance that wasn't the case."

Nile's words, the truth of them crushed Mick's resolve then. She submitted to heavy waves of sorrow that she rarely allowed an audience. On tentative steps, Nile approached, reaching out to squeeze Mick's shoulders. Cries claimed her then as well, when Mick pulled her into a clutching embrace.

"What am I supposed to do with this, Ny?" Mick queried through her sobs. "Am I supposed to rejoice because I know who my father is and that deep down he and my mother really did love me? Or am I supposed to despair in the fact that I'm the product of *two* monsters? Guilty of unspeakable crimes against children, two dregs so depraved that protecting their sick way of life was more important than pulling their own kid out of hell?"

Michaela's voice had settled to a barely audible sob as she spoke her questions. Nile merely rocked her through it all and was content to do so. Mick had other plans and was soon trying to free herself from their embrace.

"I need to get out of here-"

"Not on your own."

"Let go of me, Nile."

"No," Nile gave Mick a fast shake and then another one for good measure. "I'm going to get the keys from Taurus and you and me will get out of here. Together. No more of this loner stuff. You have a sister, remember?"

The words gave Michaela pause, anxiety and pain seeming to clear from her eyes. Nodding, her shoulders slumped and she took refuge in another hug.

~CHAPTER FOURTEEN~

Carlos found Dena on the window seat that gave a prime view of the tall, chinaberry bushes that ran the perimeter of their property. He could only hazard a guess at how long she'd been up. He had tried to fight sleep after their guests left the night before. Dena had seemed drained, but sleep didn't appear to be in demand. Carlos had managed to get her to come to bed; his plan to hold her until she drifted off. She hadn't drifted off. At least, she hadn't before he did. When he woke, she was gone.

"Coffee still hot, Babe?" He called, gracing his wife with a lazy grin and wink when he walked into the kitchen.

"Yeah…" her smile was weak. "Los? Can I ask you something?"

"Whatever you want," he encouraged, selecting a massive mug for his coffee.

"I don't want you to take it wrong..."

The lazy grin soured when he grimaced. "You should ask me anyway, otherwise my mood might take a wrong turn."

"I believe Mick could hate me after last night. Wait," she spotted the tightening of the muscles defining Carlos' bare back and knew he was about to argue her point. "She's still coming to grips with what she's already learned about her mother and now...here's this new barrel of horrors-that really could just be some sort of insane coincidence and with Cufi Muhammad of all people being her father." Dena sighed as though the recap had exhausted her.

"I could easily hate someone for putting something like that in my head," she curled her legs up on the window seat when Carlos sat next to her.

"What do you want to ask me?" He drew her feet onto his lap.

Dena grazed her thumbnail across her bottom lip for a few moments, studying her husband as if she thought the exercise would give her the answers she sought.

"It was kind of fortunate- you already having a lot of the details about my past." She fixed her gaze past the window when he lifted his probing one to her face. "All I really had to do was fill in some blanks."

"Yeah...but there were still a lot of blanks."

"But it wasn't like I'd just hit you with this."

Carlos fixed on caressing her feet. His rough palms supplied a soothing friction that made Dena lean her head on the window and sigh her contentment.

"So you want to know if I could have accepted it or whether I would've walked away?"

"Could you?" She pulled her head from the window. "Could you have accepted it? Hearing it fresh and with no previous knowledge or insight about what was up for discussion?"

"Honestly?"

"Please."

His soft greens chased the path his hand made along the dark shapeliness of her calf. Carlos smiled taking great enjoyment in the stark contrasts of their skin tones. "The truth of it D, is that I don't know how I would have reacted." His hand firmed on her thigh when his fingers began their disappearing act beneath the hem of her gown.

"I'd like to say that my love for you would have surpassed anything and that I never would have judged you for doing what you had to- mistake or no." He rested his head back on the windows, one strong shoulder rolling upwards in a lax shrug.

"I'd like to think I'm a bigger man than that, but it's not every day a husband learns such things about his wife."

Dena nodded, her eyes remaining downcast.

"You ready for another truth?" He gathered her close, a seamless move that tucked her into the wall of sinew and unyielding bone that was his chest.

"This was the *only* way it could've worked out- the way it was intended to."

"You really believe that?" Her voice was a whisper, her fist set defiantly against his breastbone.

He brushed a kiss across her knuckles and regarded them for a moment. "I do when I think back over everything we were before all this…came down on us and how your actions laid a path that I followed." He swallowed noticeably unused to succumbing to bouts of emotion.

"That path turned up a lot of ugly truths any one of 'em could've made me take the nearest detour and push you out of my head…I couldn't do that and here we are." He gave her a little tug. "We love each other, fought for each other despite all that. I think that everything that's happened-happened the only way it could have for us to be here like this now." His light eyes took on a smoldering intensity even as his mouth curved into a grin that was equally guileless and beckoning.

"I guess that's a pretty sappy outlook, but I'll take it. I love you."

Dena laughed shakily, but happily- delighted by the simplicity with which he shared the confession. "I'll take it too," tears sprinkled her cheeks. "I love you." She pressed into him, her hands lightly cupping his jaw while she kissed him.

The gesture was a display of sweetness and love. Yet; as was the way with most of their intimate moments, desire and heat weaved their lusty threads amidst those sensations. Carlos secured her neck in a loose cuff, stilling her for the exploration that began with a damp outline his tongue traced about her kissable mouth.

The exploration progressed, teasing the even ridge of her teeth before engaging her tongue. Dena shifted in his lap, whimpering when she felt him stiffen beneath her bottom. Impatiently, she wriggled herself there, the gauzy material of the mauve shift she'd worn to bed, inched higher until it was barely covering her thighs. She wore nothing beneath it. A gasp resounded in the kitchen when her bare sex hummed next to the cottony fabric of the sleep pants, low slung at his hips.

Without breaking the hungry kiss, Carlos captured her thighs. He lifted her to straddle his lap as he eased over to the middle of the cushioned window seat. He expelled relatively no exertion with the effort that only deepened Dena's desperation to have his body join hers.

Carlos suddenly broke their kiss, leaning away to take in her face as though he were in wonder of it. The pale, hypnotic orbs drifted down to where her breasts heaved and protruded beyond the lacy tassels securing the bodice of the gown.

"Take this off," he smiled when she made no move to work with the tassels.

Instead, she crossed her arms over her middle and pulled the garment up over her head. Her dark eyes were transfixed on the rugged beauty of his face while her lingerie drifted to the floor.

"Neighbors might see," she teased, challenge filtering her gaze.

"They're seven acres away." He freed the erection that throbbed almost painfully even against the loose fitting pants. "And do you really think I give a damn?" The query was little more than a rumble of sound within his chest.

Dena offered a scant toss of her head in reply and he appraised the healthy swing of glossy ebony about her dark and exquisite face. He scooped her bottom into the possessive cradle of his palms. Spreading the full, supple

194

globes he hissed an appreciative curse as her sex enveloped his in a mesmerizing well of moisture.

"That's it," he approvingly murmured, resting his head back on the wide pane of glass.

"Mmm hmm," Dena's approving moan was a bit less steady. She laid her palms flat on the window, taking great pleasure in the sensation of being stretched and filled almost to the point of being overwhelmed. The sensation was one she could not describe had her life depended on it. It was also a sensation comprised of more than physical perfection.

The fact that the man was built like a mountain was enough to make swooning an understandable reaction. Still, to have such power tempered by compassion and a love reserved only for her, sent Dena right past swooning and down the road to elation.

There was the softest of squeaks as her fingers squelched down from the spotless picture window to settle on his pronounced pectoral muscles. She marveled over the erotic image cast by their upper bodies; her nipples bumping the enviable sculpting of his chest.

Carlos relinquished his caressing hold on her derriere to capture a breast that had tempted him a bit too long. Lengthy, sleek brows drew close over his spell-casting stare the moment the satiny peaks grazed his tongue. He suckled as if famished. Surrendering his grasp on a pert mound of flesh, he braced a hand between her shoulder blades; the pressure then drawing her closer. Keeping her near, he steadily nurtured himself on the sensitized bud that firmed between his teeth.

Dena's breath came in shuddery pants mingled with weak cries that must have stirred Carlos' arousal to a higher level. Her breath hitched when he throbbed and tensed more vigorously inside her. The potency of it held her full attention until his free hand rested at the crease of her thigh. The move put his thumb in range of the extra-sensitive nub of flesh just above her femininity.

He subjected that part of her anatomy to a sensual manipulation. The pressure sent Dena convulsing on relentless waves of lust.

"Carlos," his name was a sob on her swollen lips. The effects of his triple massage had their way with every nerve ending that fired through her.

Dena was in danger of bringing an end to the sensational encounter too soon. Every so often, Carlos would squeeze her thighs urging her to still. All the while, he appeared to be summoning calm, closing his eyes and willing his hormones to cool their ferocious thundering.

Eventually, stifling Dena's moves or pulling her completely off the glistening rock solid length of his shaft, were unthinkable acts. Carlos nuzzled his gorgeous face between her breasts and allowed fulfillment to have its way.

Dena was altogether drained by the many times he'd brought her to climax. Yet she was no less enraptured by his release dousing her walls.

Gently, they re-engaged their kiss. Dena milked his shaft intent on withdrawing every ounce of his seed until he was limp and sated.

They drifted from their high together, woven into a secure cocoon as their breathing slowed. Only then, did

Carlos leave the window seat. He took Dena with him as they wordlessly returned to the bedroom.

***

Persephone James glanced up from her menu in time to see SyBilla approaching their table at the street side café where they'd agreed to meet for breakfast. Giving a tug to the maroon scarf she wore, Persephone stood and went to meet the woman she'd grown closer to over the last several weeks despite her intentions to keep her distance.

"Thanks for meeting me, SyBilla." Persephone extended both her hands.

"I'm the one who should be thanking you," Bill accepted the double handshake. "Flying all the way out here to Napa *and* locating one of our hundreds of out of the way places to eat too? Impressive."

Persephone smirked. "Yeah, I've been told my location skills border on supernatural." She teased.

"Explains how you found my cousin and his wife in France," Bill noted, reaching for the menu in the woven condiment basket.

Persephone didn't take the comment with as much amusement as it was given. "What do you think my chances are of talking to Fernando and Contessa about that in person?"

"Probably better than you think," Bill smiled up at the waiter who'd approached the table. "I don't think we'll be able to keep that from the guys in my family much longer." She said once the server had left with their orders.

"My family situation is becoming a bit strained as well," Persephone worked shaking fingers through the walnut brown locks streaking her otherwise onyx hair, her remarkable silver stare clouded with unrest. "My mother's getting to the age where she wants to right the wrongs of her past. Considering the state of her relationship with my sister, my guess is that she wants to correct that."

"Does your mother know where Evangela is?" Bill queried.

"I doubt it, but I can't be sure and I can't risk her doing anything that might lead that fool to me and my girls," Persephone reclined in the cushioned chair she occupied, crossing her long legs at the ankles.

"It wasn't easy finding a place for us." Persephone shook her head on the memories. "It'd be near to impossible this time-before I was pregnant now I've got two five year olds to contend with."

Bill dropped a hand over Persephone's to stop her fidgeting. "What can I do?"

Persephone studied Bill's hand on hers. "I know some of your job requires hiding people with...sensitive information. I was hoping to secure that service for me and my girls."

SyBilla inclined her head. "Not your mom?"

Persephone was already shaking her head. "Best I leave her settled where she is. Maybe...later after all this is done I could...I have to put the girls first. Money's not an issue, but I need someplace safe."

"And in return?" Bill's gray eyes narrowed in challenge. "what do I get in return?"

"I can't charge you all with keeping my secrets. It was wrong of me especially after everything I've done."

"Perse-"

"It's time, SyBilla. It's long past time that I see Hill and tell him." She mopped her face in her hands. "I should've never kept it."

"You were doing what was best for your kids."

"This *is* best for them," Persephone gave a resolved sigh. "You arrange the meet and I'll be there. I'll tell him everything so we can all get on to crushing the rest of this and move on with our lives."

"This is the right decision, Persephone." Bill tugged the sleeve of Persephone's navy blouse. "If he finds out any other way, he'll be too difficult to handle."

"Hmph," Persephone fiddled with the handle of her coffee cup. "You don't know Hill Tesano very well, do you? He's always been difficult to handle. When I tell him this, he's going to be downright impossible."

In spite of it all, Bill couldn't resist giving into a genuine smile. Moments later, the server was arriving with biscuits and jam to start off their breakfast.

Neither woman could've guessed that the topic of their conversation was seated in a dark truck down the street from the café. Hilliam Tesano studied SyBilla at length before his ebony stare eased over to cast a slow rake across Persephone while he wondered over what she was doing there.

***

"Un-Kay!" Quincee Mahalia Ramsey's hazy gray eyes beamed as vibrantly as her plump, dark face when her father opened the door to his brother that morning.

"There's my baby doll," Quaysar Ramsey took his niece from his twin, bouncing the bubbly little girl a few times before he set a kiss to her tiny bow mouth. Keeping the child close, he focused on Quest. "Does Daddy need a kiss too?" He teased.

"Daddy," Always in the mood for kisses, Quincee puckered her mouth in her father's direction.

Quest obliged without hesitation. "Thanks Cocoa Puff," he put another kiss to his daughter's temple.

"Where's Mommy?" Quay gave his niece another little bounce.

"Mommy sleeping, shh…" Quincee spoke quietly and placed a short, chubby finger to her lips to encourage silence.

"Why are *you* up and at 'em so early?" Quest asked his brother.

Unfairly lengthy lashes feathered down over Quay's dark eyes when he sighed. "When Tyke asked if I had a meeting- three times in a row- I figured she was telling me to get out in her own sweet way."

Quest chuckled, thinking of his sister-in-law. Tykira would be delivering twin girls to the Ramsey line soon. Quest's amusement however faded far too quickly.

"How's she doin'?" Quay glanced toward the front stairway.

Quest followed his brother's gaze. "I went to bed after I talked to you and she didn't wake me when she got in so…I'm not sure."

"And how are you?" Quay brushed a kiss across Quincee's forehead. The little girl was busy inspecting the buttons on the long-sleeved oak shirt he wore and not on the conversation between he and Quest. Quay glimpsed the despair he'd already sensed and knew his twin was doing his best to hide.

"I keep thinking I should've..."

"What? Kept this quiet? Hidden to protect her? You knew that was out of your hands the second you heard it and it would've *killed* Dena to hold onto it and Mick would've *killed* you for trying to hide it." Quay cooled his voice on the word *killed* so as not to rouse Quincee's attention. "You're gonna have to let this play out, man. There's a chance it's not even true."

Quest muttered a curse. "It's true alright...just another in a long stream of crazy revelations I've come to expect."

"Even still, you're gonna have to let the chips fall, man."

"And if this destroys her?" Quest looked at his brother as though he were a stranger. "Knowing why they left her and decided to raise Nile instead?"

"She's tougher than that and you know it."

"Mommieee!" Quincee's voice echoed in the foyer when she saw Michaela on the stairway.

"Hey girl! Sleepin' in?" Quay called.

"I was tryin' to before I heard *your* big mouth," Mick grumbled playfully, tightening her robe's belt while crossing the foyer to the trio.

"Ouch," Quay replied while Mick kissed Quincee's cheek and then drew him down for the same treatment.

"How's Ty?" She asked.

"Mean." Quay flatly supplied. "But treatin' the boys like kings, fussin' all over 'em and stuff." He said of his and Ty's adopted sons Dinari and Dakari. "Ma says she's nurturing or something."

Mick laughed. "*Nesting.*"

201

"What's that mean?" Quay scowled.

"Means you're gonna have two of these real soon," Mick tugged on the hem of Quincee's pink T-shirt.

Quest had kept quiet during the morning greetings. He felt his heart seize when Michaela finally looked his way.

"Can I talk to you?" She asked him.

"Hey?" Quay gave Quincee yet another bounce. "Can we go play?" He asked her.

"Yaaaay!" The little girl cheered amidst a tumble of giggles.

"Her dolls and stuff are in my office," Quest told his brother.

Uncle and Niece set off while Mick returned to the staircase. She ascended and took a seat on the landing to wait on Quest to join her. When he did, he wasted no time getting the conversation underway.

"Did I screw up again?"

Mick's expression softened another level. "Baby no…" she soothed, pulling him close. "No…" she rocked him a bit, feeling his faint shuddering in her arms. "You did good." She peppered a few kisses to his jaw, temple and forehead.

"But how do you feel knowing all this?"

"I don't know," Mick raised a brow. "There's a chance it's not even true. Just death bed ramblings from some lunatic. Even if it *is* true, it really only proves that Nile was a truer sister than she already was."

"And the fact that they raised her instead of you?"

"Hard to swallow," she nodded. "It'd probably be impossible to swallow were it not for the fact that my life,"

202

everything in it-good or bad got me here. *Here* in *this* life with you and our girl." Michaela leaned into the hard kiss Quest was suddenly searing into her neck.

"A part of me is…I don't know…at ease with knowing-maybe that she *did* leave to protect me in her own way and he-did want me at least…a little, but Quest I honestly believe that had one thing turned out differently, we wouldn't be here together. And that, my love, would be the real tragedy." She nuzzled her nose into the flawless dark chocolate perfection of his cheek.

Their lips melded sweetly at first and then Quest was crushing her mouth beneath his.

"Let me take you back to bed," he said while taking her mouth with his dreamy intensity.

"Mmm…but I'm not sleepy."

"Good."

She exhaled a laugh. "Stop. Pike and Belle-"

"Still in bed and in the wing on the other side of the house, remember?" Quest said of his cousin and her husband who had opted to stay on a little longer following the holiday trip. Belle wanted more time to see Fernando.

"Quay's here." Mick said.

"Quinn's got her tea-set down there." Quest nodded meaningfully when his wife's amber stare lit up with hope.

Almost everyone in the family had been a guest for one of Quincee Ramsey's tea parties. The events were known to run close to an hour.

"He can use all the tea party experience he can get, right?" Quest commenced to nibbling Mick's ear.

"You're willing to let him have *all* that fun? Couldn't you use a little more experience?" She purred.

"I'm good."

"Mmm…I don't know…Quinn may have to share that set soon and we may all be invited to a whole new round of parties."

Quest's ear-nibbling stopped. He pulled back. But for the slight furrow forming between his long, satiny brows, he was otherwise still.

Mick pretended not to notice. "You've gone and done it again Mr. Ramsey. I'm pregnant."

Quest's gray eyes; darkened then by an emotion other than anger, fell to her stomach. "The holiday trip?"

"Before that- I think before Scotland maybe but then everything went haywire. I didn't get around to confirming everything 'til little over a week ago. I was coming to tell you that morning Taurus came by to talk about Dena- the time didn't seem right. I don't know…hey, what were we saying about being first with all the news?"

Her attempt at playfulness didn't rub off on Quest. "Are you alright with this." His dark stare was fixed, probing. "During the trip you said-"

"I know," she tapped fingers to her brow and nodded. "I know and I meant it, but the day I got it all confirmed I- somehow it didn't matter anymore." She balled her hands in the folds of her robe.

"If I had another doubt, it vanished after last night. Nile was right there for me," she smiled on the memory. "She wouldn't let me drive off on my own. She held me when I cried, let me rage and ramble- it wasn't pretty. I want Quincee to know what it's like to have someone who's got your back, who understands without you ever having to explain it, you know?"

"Yeah...Yeah I do," Quest thought of Quay then.

"She'll never be alone-she's gonna be blessed with an ample supply of cousins to keep her company. Now she's going to be blessed with something greater."

"I love you," Quest murmured the words against her mouth while he lifted Mick high.

"I love you." Michaela initiated a kiss as they continued their ascent up the stairs.

***

Dena McPhereson spent the morning in bed with her husband and then returned to the kitchen. Carlos was still asleep so she decided to prepare a late lunch for them to enjoy. The day was overcast and promised rain before nightfall. She figured soup and sandwiches would go over just fine. She was taking an inventory of the stock in her soup cabinet when the doorbell rang.

Dena hurried to the front, not wanting the ring to wake Carlos. She pulled open the heavy door without thinking, stunned by who waited on the other side.

"Mick? What-Are you okay?" Dena's lashes feathered down over her eyes. "Stupid question."

"Can I come in?" Mick sighed.

"Yes, yes, yes," Dena stepped aside quickly waving Mick forward.

"I was um-just starting lunch a-a late lunch..." Unnerved by the damage she believed she'd done to one of her best friends, Dena began to ramble. "It's only soup and sandwiches. The weather calls for it today, don't you think?" She tossed a quick smile over her shoulder. "I don't know what soup is best. Do you want to stay?"

Michaela caught the long sleeve of Dena's casual T-shirt dress. "I only want one thing, right now." She spread her arms. "Can I have a hug?"

Tears made an instant appearance, pooling and glistening in Dena's bottomless eyes. Giving in to her sobs, she joined Michaela for a lengthy embrace.

~~~

"I felt like I owed you. Had you not come into our lives, determined to find out what happened to Sera, I don't know if anything would've gotten me back to Seattle."

Mick topped off their coffees. They had gone back to the kitchen where Dena brewed a pot of her coveted hazelnut roast which they enjoyed from the small round table facing the terrace and back lawn then being drenched by the promised downpour.

"Carlos would've gotten you back here." Mick predicted.

Dena smiled while shaking her head. "Not as long as all this was hanging over my head. I was sure I could hide it from everybody but him. Hmph, then I find out he knew most of it all along. How insane is that?" She dragged her fingers through her hair.

"Fate's a strange and captivating thing."

"You can say that again," Dena grinned over Mick's outlook.

"You're always talking about what you *owe* everyone." Michaela absently stirred her coffee. "Sounds like you've forgotten about what *you're* owed."

"Me?" Dena proffered a minute shake of her head.

"Evangela told you why she wanted Belle, right?"

"Because of Mr. Jasper."

"A.K.A. Eston Perjas."

"I still can't believe that, but I know it's true."

Mick leaned closer to the table. "Aren't you curious? To confront the-the creator of the place that spawned Evangela and her madness?"

Dena managed another smile. "Eva was mad long before that island."

Mick laughed. "I won't argue that. But...Honey now that we know who he is...it's only right and fair for him to help us fill in some of the blanks."

Dena pushed aside her mug. "I don't want to hurt Belle with this."

"Who do you think I talked to about it before I came to you?" Mick waited for Dena to look at her. "She's got questions of her own, so does Pike- his brother was there for a long time. You and Nile have every right to face the man who helped create the business that took so much from you both."

Instinctively, Dena curved her hands over her belly. "What are you suggesting?"

Michaela looked around the kitchen. "I think it's time for another family dinner."

~CHAPTER FIFTEEN~

It took well over a week of tweaking schedules and revising travel plans to put that evening's event into place. Besides all the running around for the upcoming Christmas holiday, Dena had been playing catch-up with her duties on planning her aunt Josephine's wedding to her long time love Crane Cannon.

As the McPheresons had previously opened their home for a night of revelations; that evening, it was Quest's and Michaela's turn. The rain had been a light but steady companion for over a week and showed no signs of making an exit any time soon.

It hardly mattered, Mick thought as she sat next to her husband in their living room and studied the faces of their guests. Rain and glumness often went hand in hand and glum was a perfect descriptor for each expression. Little surprise-given the purpose for the gathering. Following dinner; the contents of which Mick felt rolling in her stomach like a nervous bubble, the group shuffled into the living room.

Jasper Stone aka Eston Perjas and his new bride made the trip from Monte Carlo where they had begun the first leg of their honeymoon. They detoured to Seattle when their daughter called and told them they needed to change their plans.

Pike and Sabella would be returning to their home back east. Belle's OB/GYN would eventually deem it best for her not to travel. That being the case, the get together was a necessity as that particular group may not be assembled again for quite some time.

Sabella told her father what she knew and how important it was that he answer a few pressing questions from several interested parties. Hearing that, Jasper knew that obliging his daughter's request was the only right course of action.

With Carmen at his side, Jasper Stone began his tale that night during dinner. He started with his upbringing- the story of an outcast- the bastard child of a shameless woman and her married lover. Somehow, Michaela's succulent roast beef and cabbage stew disappeared as Jasper shared his (and Carmen's) story, much of which had not been previously revealed to some of the younger generation.

Dena, Michaela and Nile lent shocked gasps as Jasper's tale deepened. Their husbands responded with lowered heads that shook ever so often in reaction to some new and more awful part of the story.

~~~

"So he's really dead?" Dena asked leaning forward on the loveseat she shared with Carlos as she grew more enraptured by Jasper's words.

"He is, D.D.," Carmen addressed her niece. "He's really dead. I lit the match myself and watched him burn."

"Marcus was your friend?" Nile questioned Jasper. "Along with the Tesanos and our father," she looked to Michaela who sat curled into Quest on a sofa across the room. "You were friends with them all."

"I was." Jasper tilted his head a fraction in confirmation.

"How could you work with the man that-" Nile pressed her lips together when she looked to Carmen.

Jasper bowed his head then. "I didn't realized he'd gotten himself involved in it all until much later and I…" he rubbed his hand across Carmen's. "I didn't have the rest of the story until much later. I thought it was beneficial to keep an eye on the man." He gripped Carmen's hand then and squeezed. "Turns out, I was right."

"And Muhammad?" Quest's cool, rich tone filled the room next. "Why get involved with him? From what you've told us, he was no more of a friend to you in those days than Marc."

"Our involvements came later," Jasper smoothed a hand across his close cut salt and pepper hair. "Charlt made a smart move when he got into the shipping business. I like to believe he had the best intentions when he started out but," he turned sorrowful eyes upon Nile and Mick.

"He'd never been an honorable man. The quick, abundant buck was what he was loyal to."

"And you?" The edge in Carlos' voice accentuated the lethal ability barely concealed beneath his tense frame. "What were *you* loyal to?"

"My work," Jasper returned without hesitation or remorse over the fact. "The means didn't matter to me, only the ends. In the beginning it was about proving what had to be true. I was driven by the belief that what made a person evil lay in the blood. Growing up, I'd always believed that and it was hard to sway that train of thought when I heard it at every turn."

Jasper braced elbows to his knees when he leaned forward, regarding the lines in his rough palms. "My mother had no shame in the way she drew other women's men into her bed. It was easy for her, I guess. She was a beauty- you're the image of her," he looked to Belle being cradled by her husband.

"The fact that I was a child, didn't matter. People were always telling me my mother was nothing- I'd be nothing. I came to understand the word abomination at an early age. Chemistry fascinated me and I…I thought understanding it would help me find the answers to all the questions about what I was. Was I destined to be nothing because of what my mother was? And what about people like Marc and Houston? They'd come from great people like Mr. Quentin and Ms. Marcella and they were evil with no apologies."

"With all due respect, Sir, my father and uncle didn't create a place bent on destroying the lives of kids," Dena said. "Black Island was *your* brain child. Not theirs."

"What Black Island became- *is*- isn't what I intended it to be." He ran the back of his hand along his wife's thigh. "When I lost Carmen, all I had was the work I started with Dr. Dowd in Vietnam," he referenced his mentor and benefactor Army Captain Owen Dowd.

"When Dr. Dowd left me his entire estate, I was free to take that work into whole other levels of research. Things I never thought I'd be able to delve into."

"And innocent kids were the perfect guinea pigs," Taurus grated, his rage as thinly concealed as Carlos' and Dena's.

"The kids I reached out to at first were runaways- correction *throwaways*. None were cared for enough to be missed. Maybe I was naïve but I'd hoped the arrangement would be of mutual benefit." He leaned back on the loveseat he shared with Carmen, folding his arms across his chest.

"The first kids- many of whom remain part of my organization into this day- lived at the research park. They had their own rooms in houses designated for them. Those kids were blessed if they could find a box to take refuge in. I gave them a home."

"Daddy," Belle lifted her head from Pike's shoulder. "You can't believe they knew the consequences of your tests."

Jasper looked to Nile and Dena. "I don't expect you to believe it, but the management of that testing was never sanctioned by me or anyone loyal to me. As I got deeper

212

into my research," he rubbed his eyes as the weight of the story began to mount. "Running of the park became more of a chore. It was about that time when a scientist on my team introduced me to your uncle," he looked to Pike.

"Humphrey was doing work of his own with a team out of Portland. Until then, I hadn't ventured into ovarian studies. With the exception of a few young women meant to serve in a purely administrative capacity, I was content to have the island be exclusive to young men. My work focused on hematology- the study of the blood. I studied its various disorders and had no interest in changing that. Humphrey and I had similar motivations in that he was also curious about what happened inside the body- inside the cells that made a person what they are. He called it 'Perfection from Conception'."

Jasper sighed, weariness making him seem aged for the first time. "The boys were treated well on the island," he said. "Boys like your friend Kraven and your cousin Fernando," he looked to Taurus and Quest. "And your brother," he looked to his son-in-law then.

"Hill was among the first of the *non*-throwaways. He had a family out there who loved him, but he still felt misunderstood at home. Boys like your cousin Brogue. He arrived shortly before I made my departure. There was lots of potential there for better things than what he turned into but boys do tend to obsess about pleasing their fathers or any man who takes a real interest," he smirked self-indulgently. "Gives us purpose and self-worth. I believe your uncle Gabriel loved his son but something held him back from showing it so he was instead more overbearing. He told me Brogue's being there would toughen him up."

"Instead it got him killed," Pike noted, anger kindling in his voice as vibrantly as it did in his gaze.

Jasper nodded. "It got many of them killed and that wasn't what I intended. The purpose of my work was to develop enhancements to improve brain function by injecting certain specialized enzymes that would travel to areas of the brain that commanded impulsivity, inhibitions, morality-knowing right from wrong... but I then began to think of enhancements to benefit the mind *and* body."

Quiet took control of the room then. Jasper seemed to be drawing on the will to continue. He found it in the reassuring shoulder rubs Carmen supplied.

"Those boys were the catalysts for a whole new kind of motivation- strong, fast, intelligent *and* moral? They could have been unstoppable-many were. In those early days the successes far outweighed the failures."

"What constituted a failure?" Carlos asked.

"Not every mind develops the same and... modifications tended to have abhorrent results. We developed something to combat certain side effects of the studies. But Re-Gen was unstable so I phased it out of my studies."

"You know it's still being produced?"

Jasper fixed Dena with an incredulous look. "Can't be. It was specific to my work-useless otherwise."

"I've taken it. Became addicted to it," Dena exhaled, refreshed after making the admission. "It did wonders to mask certain...unpleasant dreams."

"And did it *un*mask other things?" Jasper probed. "Headaches, perhaps?" He saw the truth in her eyes. "It was one of the milder side effects of the product of which there were many-that's why I discontinued it. *One* reason why- I knew it was addictive which gave it the potential to be a cash cow- one that took quite a hold over the island before I left.

"There were some of my team who took a shine to it- found some of its properties worthy of further research. If it's still being produced that could mean they've found something to exploit. I wanted to stop the human testing altogether and go back to the drawing board. After so much success, I didn't want to chuck it all but I cared about those kids."

Jasper's face hardened and he seemed to stiffen against Carmen's shoulder rubs. "All Humphrey saw was an army with limitless possibilities. He said soldiers didn't need to be hindered by morals and ethics- leave that to those in charge and just let them take orders. He was bringing them in by the boatloads and my only concern was that I had more test subjects." He gave a self-deprecating shrug.

"Humphrey though...he reminded me that those *kids* were young men- young men whose bodies were going through all kinds of changes- who were in need of certain...physical outlets."

"We were still at odds about ovarian study, but I thought he had a point about the boys' sexual needs. I left him to handle it, not realizing I was laying the foundation for a path to my own exit. Behind my back, he was discussing his ideas with a few of the other scientists and gradually wooing them over to his way of thinking. They were good men, loyal enough to me that they came to plead Humphrey's case instead of brewing something in secret.

215

They convinced me that closing off ovarian research was a weak spot in my initiative."

Across the room, Dena traded a weighty look with Nile.

"They said if I really wanted to perform a holistic study of how one's brain formed and operated then wouldn't the study of the ovary be just as vital to that understanding as the blood? I gave them the go-ahead." Jasper clenched a fist, bumping it to his jaw.

"I was a coward. I said nothing even though none of it sat well with me. Harvesting and studying ovaries that way…it seemed dangerous- it *was* dangerous. I knew too much could go wrong." Again, he looked to Nile and Dena. "But still I said nothing, kept to my own research and the girls…so many flowed in. I never asked who they were or where they came from. Just stuck my head in the sand- just let Hump and his crew of…mad scientists," he smiled distastefully over the phrasing. "I just let them move on with their research."

Mick spoke up then. "Do you expect us to believe that you had no interest in what their research-mad or not-revealed?"

"Oh I had an interest Michaela. Just not so much in how they uncovered the findings," Jasper confessed, he watched his wife leave to top of their coffees from the table behind a long sofa.

"Did the girls have an interest?" Dena asked.

Jasper paused for a few beats. "For many of them, the bigger concern was not having to spend the night on the street or with abusive parents-foster, adoptive or biological. Having somebody cut into them for something they were too young to understand the purpose of...staying there and being subjected to that was the lesser of an evil they couldn't even recognize."

"So they were there for research and pleasure?" Belle asked.

"Humphrey decided *that* particular 'perk' would be for our...top performers." Jasper explained. "A reward and slowly the culture-the...mission of the island changed."

"And the girls got older..." Carlos pointed out.

"And they left," Jasper added, "and then someone had the bright idea that it would be wise to consider that those...non-essential island cast offs were taking with them some very essential information about what we did there."

"And the clean-up operations were born?" Pike noted, smiling coolly when his father-in-law nodded.

"The kids were always free to leave whenever they wanted- that...changed eventually but the damage had already been done. Over one hundred kids- male and female had already been through there and left with our blessings to start lives or something as close to a life as many of them could build." Jasper sipped at the coffee Carmen handed him.

"But Hump thought it was time to put our army to use and," he nodded to Pike, "the clean-up jobs were born. Those...missions gave the group an impressive resume and your uncle Stone negotiated the army's necessary talents to third world warlords, regimes, even governments- ours included."

A collective array of groans filled the room.

"Humphrey even saw a way to turn a profit with the ovarian research and presented some of the young women as surrogate mothers."

"God…" Mick bowed her head as did Belle; who looked ill besides.

"As I said, 'the culture of the island' changed."

"Evangela Leer is interested in a research park," Dena said, folding her hands in the hem of an oversized long-sleeved tee. "She says it's not on the island. It's why she wanted me to bring Belle to her- to encourage you to share what you know about it."

"Unless she's talking about my place in Mozambique, I have no leads," Jasper's mouth curved into a sneer. "If she'd like to pay a visit to Vilanculous, my staff and I would happily give her a proper welcome."

"Evangela's been at this a long time." Dena said. "Everyone she's ever gone after had earned a spot on that death list of hers. Whatever she's looking for, she's not of a mind to share it and it's about a lot more than re-stocking her supply of Re-Gen. She'll go through anyone to get it."

"How much was she involved with you and the Tesanos?" Carlos asked.

"She was among the few girls who worked the island in admin capacities." Jasper explained. "At first she could've been doing anything, maybe shuttling correspondence between me and my research team across the island. As things became more…involved her duties varied. One week she could've been overseeing new arrivals and the next she could've been coordinating meet and greets for interested… investors. Those were more abundant following Gabe's and Vale's joining."

"My uncles run it all now, don't they?" Pike asked.

"*Vale* runs it all and Gabe…well he found himself in the very position he condemned his son. Even though their father was alive, he and Vale saw Humphrey as more of a father figure- the one whose approval they wanted. For some reason, Gabe could never get it, but Vale, Hump welcomed with open arms. Perhaps he saw in Vale that perverse nature that he never wanted to fully tap into himself."

"So he left Vale to do the dirty work," Taurus said.

Jasper smiled. "While Gabe's interests were less about Black Island business and more Tesano related, Vale was immersed in the workings of the island. Because it was a secret association, no one really saw Vale as having any sort of power or influence. Everybody just assumed Gabe was at the head of it all. Hump took time to teach his youngest brother that true power lay *behind* the curtains."

Carlos' observations of Jasper grew less rigid and he leaned forward. "What was the final straw for you? Did Vale put changes in place that were too outrageous even for you?"

Jasper seemed stricken by the question. Quickly, his head bowed and he reached for his wife's hand to squeeze.

"Carmen and I grew up in a different time." He told the younger people in the room. "It was a time when things were more…overt. People had a problem with you, they said so and you could either duke it out, walk away or both. Not like now where it seems there's more security in subtly- telling someone how you feel about them-*really* feel by using the cover of anonymity as your shield. In *that*-Humphrey Tesano was ahead of his time. Not only did he preach about the power being *behind* the curtain, he lived it. Before leaving the island, I realized just how much."

Jasper kissed the back of Carmen's hand as if to thank her for its reassuring grip. "Of course," he continued, "Hump had little choice there since his interests ran far outside his field of expertise. To explore them, he needed the help of others. At first, he could barely articulate what he wanted, but his charisma and money effectively masked those ineptitudes.

"As he gained more information and became more literate, he understood that it'd be in his best interest to still not *fully* articulate until he'd found a group of like-minded professionals."

"Your scientists," Dena guessed.

"Mmm," Jasper added a nod to the confirmation. "What I had at Black Island provided the perfect set up, but as I said- ovarian studies wasn't where I wanted to take my research. Eventually, I saw the logic in doing so and together Hump and I may have uncovered vast amounts of vital knowledge. Instead, I uncovered that our interests weren't fueled by the same motivations after all." Jasper passed his empty coffee mug to Carmen who dutifully refilled it.

"Should we take a break?" Mick asked, looking toward Belle.

Soon everyone's eyes were fixed on one of the two expectant moms in the room. Belle merely shook her head on Pike's shoulder where she'd rested since the onset of the conversation. The warm pecan brown of her gaze fired with determination.

"No, I want to finish this," she said.

"So do I." Dena added, her eyes never veering from her cousin's father.

Jasper seemed ready to continue as well, quieting until Carmen returned with yet another refilled mug. He savored the coffee's flavor and aroma before moving on.

"I don't know if Humphrey Tesano ever asked himself if what he wanted to...set in motion was highly improbable but he was a wealthy man, able to fund highly improbable research to span a multitude of lifetimes."

"What did he want?" Nile's voice was a whisper that seemed to resound in the room.

"We all know that genes, ovaries, sperm help to supply the coding-the instructions that help to make us who we are." Jasper cleared his throat; for the first time he seemed hesitant. "Humphrey wondered if those instructions could be...*managed* in some way to dictate race."

"Bullshit," Quest blurted amidst a slew of gasps, groans and muffled oaths among the group.

"No doubt," Jasper agreed, "But it was what the man believed. He believed it with such conviction that he was able to sway those who should have known better."

Belle was then sitting up instead of leaning on her husband. "How do you know all this Daddy?"

"By way of a disagreement I had with one of the other doctors on staff. As I said, Hump was a very convincing character which enabled him to incite a passion in some that nothing could cool."

"Except researching something so deranged." Taurus chimed in.

"And they were fully on board to do that." Jasper set his mug to the end table next to the loveseat. "I went to confront Humphrey and; while he wasn't pleased to have the secret revealed, he didn't deny it. Told me he'd seen babies white as snow come from women black as tar and he wanted to know how that could be? How did darkness have the power to create or overcome light on a whim- especially in the womb? Could that occurrence be changed? Commanded? Imagine the possibilities: wealthy, white, barren couples provided with their very own white babies; ovaries and sperm provided by white or non-white biological parents already in residence on the island. Cash cow indeed."

"He was insane." Pike breathed.

"And driven," Jasper added, "He admitted to me that his drive was motivated by your uncle Pitch. His mother was a black woman, I believe. That drive was elevated when his brother Roman had his boys- you and your brothers. He sounded in awe when he spoke of you all. He was obsessed with knowing how a dark-skinned thing like Imani could deliver sons so like the Tesanos in every way. He most wanted to understand how that one flaw of darkness was heightened in Smoak and not in the rest of you given that you all came from the same womb."

"Flaw," Nile repeated.

"Yes, his words," Jasper smiled indulgently. "I had a problem with that term myself-solved it with my fist to his jaw. He retaliated by telling me that *he* was in charge but that much I already knew. I didn't belong there anymore. I left, letting him think he'd defeated me and he was arrogant enough to think his words would make me cower and accept.

"I packed my entire lab that night and left my home like *I* was the imposter." Jasper retrieved his mug. "I spent several years trying to re-establish myself, several more trying to forget what I left and what I left it to. I worked to devise a way to destroy the place, but when I went back all I found was an army boot camp-soldiers and trainers. No trace of the research labs or personnel at all."

"You're sure?" Carlos asked.

"I knew the place like the back of my hand. I'm sure enough."

"Army boot camp or not, it's coming down." Pike vowed.

"That was my plan. We'd hoped that by putting the island under surveillance, it would tell us what was really going on but there was nothing. And then I had more important things to devote my time to," he kissed the back of Carmen's hand.

Pike massaged the bridge of his nose. "Maybe Vale isn't such an idiot after all."

"And that's the really bad news," Jasper scowled. "He's smart and holds all the keys. The good news is that he *does* hold all the keys and when one commands such power there's always someone waiting in the wings to tear it all down." He left his seat then, choosing to refill his own mug.

"Do what you have to, to bring it down," Jasper urged over his shoulder. "But before you do, be sure you're destroying the *entire* creature and not just a part that could easily grow back."

~CHAPTER SIXTEEN~

Jasper's willingness to share extended the conversation well past midnight. Eventually, sheer exhaustion; added to the fact that Jasper Stone had been questioned, re-questioned and questioned again, brought an end to the tension-abundant evening.

Carmen Ramsey Stone said her goodnights to her family and then left with her husband. It was understood and accepted that the couple was definitely entitled to a getaway of their own.

Quest and Michaela would accommodate Pike and Belle for a few more weeks before the Tesanos made their way back east. Taurus and Nile joined the two couples-there was no chatter. The six merely drew solace from one another while continuing to absorb all they had learned that night.

Carlos and Dena didn't join the others. Instead they'd claimed space on the other side of the airy sitting room. They shared the settee on the terrace that faced Quest's and Mick's west lawn.

Having held his wife for the better part of fifteen minutes, Carlos felt it was time to take a serious survey of her mood. Giving her a squeeze, he nuzzled her ear until she squirmed and angled up to brush her mouth across his angular jaw.

"Are you good?" His tone was playfully gruff.

Dena turned, snuggled back into him while she nodded. "That might change once I'm done absorbing all this."

"Understood." Carlos kissed the top of her head.

"He was right, you know?"

"How so?"

"What Mr. Jasper said about the kids not realizing what was being done or..." she bristled, "*taken* from them. The ones that *did* know, probably didn't care- lesser of two evils and all that."

He nodded against her head. "Could be," he said.

"But I think I *did* know, Carlos. I mean, there was something wrong with that place and what they were trying to explain was going to happen...I let it happen anyway."

"Hey?" He squeezed, giving her a tiny jerk in the process. "You were a child like all the rest of them."

"But I had a family. I went back to my life while those others- that *became* their life and I don't feel guilty over something I had no control over," she gave a hasty

225

wave of one hand. "But tonight I realized that in my…search to repay some debt my father owed, all I'd really done was help someone fulfill a personal vendetta: one that had done nothing to put an end to a very sick group of people except pave the way for another to take its place."

Carlos smoothed his cheek against hers. "What Stone said about destroying the entire creature?" He waited for her nod. "We will, D. I promise you, we will."

~~~

"Are you okay with this, Bella?"

Sabella and Pike occupied one of the two long sofas that ran parallel along the mosaic print rug that was then littered with almost eight pairs of shoes. The group had joined before the fire and were discussing how best to move forward.

For a time, Belle rested against her husband considering his question while she focused on the navy, wine and hunter green colors that weaved through the large rug.

"I'm sure," she sighed, "I think I've heard about all the secrets I can stand."

"Amen," Nile and Mick spoke in synchronized sighs before joining in with the soft laughter that followed among the others.

"To err on the side of caution, Hon," Dena said even though she'd nodded her agreement with Belle, "You're just now starting a relationship with him- things are bound to get tense with all the input we'll ask him to give as we try to end this thing. I'm talking about Caiphus and Bill. They're family and they're also…"

No one really needed for Dena to finish the statement.

"They work under the notion that their efforts will achieve justice where people pay for their crimes." She said. "They may require that of your dad and their payment may be steep."

"I think he's tired of hiding from it." Belle said. "I don't think he'll just surrender to whatever justice is deemed necessary, not before he does everything in his power to make things right- to make sure me and Mama are safe. I also believe he knows it's time to face what he put in motion- even if it jeopardizes the life he wants, was cheated out of having with my mother and me."

Belle sounded strong enough, but Pike could feel her shuddering. He merely tightened his embrace to shelter her with warmth.

~~~

"Where to?" Carlos asked as he wrapped Dena in the jacket she'd worn that evening. They were preparing to leave Quest's and Mick's. Taurus and Nile left shortly after Pike and Belle went upstairs to bed.

"Home please," Dena propped her chin on the middle of his chest and looked at him in a dreamy manner. "With all the cherries in the world on top."

"You got it," he finished bundling her into the jacket and then bundled her into a hug.

227

"'Los?" her voice was muffled, but still carried. "Are you going to try and keep me out of the rest of this?"

"Hmm..." Carlos pretended to think it over momentarily. "I'm guessing that'd piss you off. Am I right?"

"Damn right."

"Right. So I'm thinking it'd be pretty stupid of me to piss off a woman who can put me on my ass."

Dena hid her face in his chest to muffle the wave of laughter that bubbled up her throat. She sobered a tad after a few moments. "I guess you do have brains to go with all that beauty after all, huh?"

Carlos gave a mocking shrug of defeat. "I'm used to being misunderstood."

"Poor baby," she cupped his jaw, pulled him down into a kiss.

"So...home?" He said when she let him up for air.

"Home."

"What are we gonna do there?"

Dena pretended to mull it over. "Anything that requires us to be in our birthday suits," she suggested.

"Ah...I know the perfect thing."

"See? Not all brawn by a long shot."

***

One Week Later~

Laughter. The dream always started with laughter...ended in a blood red haze. The king sized bed creaked its protests beneath Maeva Leer's thrashing body. Comforter, blanket and sheets had been wrestled to the floor long ago.

"Get…off her," the growling chant had become Mae's litany during the nightmare/memory which gained volume as it often did the closer her dream churned towards its end.

Hand clenched into a chunky fist, Mae punched her own cheek, the top of her head, her abdomen. At last, she was awake, panting and washed in sweat. She swiped moisture from her mouth with the back of her hand while jackknifing from the bed to storm for the closed door.

She lost her footing the moment she stepped out into the hallway and hit her head on the polished hardwoods. Mae levered herself up on one elbow and began to assess her surroundings.

The sticky, metallic ooze was the first giveaway. The blood coating her palm wasn't part of a dream. Something was very wrong and were there any lingering doubts, she need only to look towards the end of the hall where the lifeless bodies of her colleagues lay in a bloody tangle.

Crawling and slip-sliding in the pooled blood that smeared her PJs, Mae looked down into the faces of Lula Velez and Santi Dumont. Santi's blonde hair appeared a grotesque yellow orange in the moonlight when it streamed her locks.

In the next moment, Mae felt her breathing hindered by the beefy arm locked beneath her jaw. The hold bent her head back at a painful angle. Not until she grunted- a result of discomfort and rage- did the pressure release. A fist to the back of her head sent Mae face first into the flooring. She was jerked up by her collar, her jaw wrenched into a crushing hold. Lips brushed her ear before hot breath followed.

"Keep your trap shut big bitch or we'll have to lower our standards and give you what we gave them before they bit the dust."

Male chuckling followed. More than one male, Mae deduced.

"Doubt she'll get anything out of it," One man said before joining his colleagues in another round of laughs.

"Move," the man holding Mae's jaw ordered, yanking her to her feet.

~~~

"How long will you be?"

"Not very. You just be awake when I get there."

"Then you better not take too long to get here."

There was laughter between the newlyweds. Jasper Stone rested his head back on the passenger seat of the Hummer he occupied.

"Jas-"

"Shh…" he urged his wife, hearing her concern, the veiled note of caution in her tone. "I know," he said.

"We should've told them," Carmen worried.

"Another long sticky story best saved for another time and a much larger audience."

Carmen's sigh rushed through the phone at her husband's words. "You're right. You're right."

There was a hand to Jasper's shoulder. A man dressed in black fatigues and garbed with gun holsters and knife belts stood just inside the open door.

"We're good to go, Sir," he said.

Jasper's singular nod sent the man on his way. "I love you," he said to Carmen through the phone.

"I love you." She said in turn.

~~~

"This is quite lovely. I've never considered property in Portugal."

"You're a dead man," Evangela sneered. She bristled, but would not give the men restraining her, the satisfaction of hearing her sob in pain when their grips tightened on her shoulders.

Jasper squatted before Evangela where his men had her on her knees. The groan she'd fought to stifle, surfaced when he closed his hand over her throat.

"Then death will be something we'll have in common little girl," he brought her face closer so she could see his snarl, feel his breath hitting her skin. "That you even dared to *speak* my child's name is all the motivation I need to crush your neck. But then, you threaten her too?"

"I never-" Eva gagged when Jasper began to make good on his threat.

"Threatening my girl is cause enough to take my men up on their enthusiastic offers to show you the time of your life in this…safe house of yours before they kill you." He nodded then, the gesture a silent instruction to his men to release their hold on Evangela. Smiling, he waited for the flood of words he knew she'd been smothering.

But for the sheen of uncertainty in her gaze, Eva was otherwise undaunted. "You men and your threats of sexual humiliation- hollow if it weren't for your strength."

"Strength is only part of it, bitch." One of Jasper's men boasted overhead. He placed his groin in direct line of Eva's sight to clarify his meaning.

A second later, he joined Eva on his knees once she had planted her fist between his legs. For her trouble, she received a backhanded blow to her face.

"Stand down!" Jasper ordered.

"Why is better, stronger, faster only relevant when we speak of men, Captain?" Eva retaliated, her mouth glossy with blood from a split lip.

"What are you after?" Jasper regarded her closely.

"A piece of the pie," she grimaced when the men secured their restraining holds. "I think I've earned it after all these years."

"So go back to the island and claim it."

"Fuck that place! Nothing more than a soldier's paradise. Nothing of value, like all that research. What's become of it, Perjas? You must've at least kept track of your wayward researchers. Where'd they go when you went into hiding from the Tesanos?!"

"I didn't hide." Jasper spoke slowly, watching Evangela more curiously then. "I dared any of them to show up on my doorstep. I'll pay for the business we conducted, but the Tesanos had no part in my studies after I left the island. Neither did the researchers I collaborated with."

"Please," Evangela spat out a stream of blood that had congealed at her swollen lip. "You think I'm talking about that little kingdom of yours in Mozambique?"

Jasper stood, his expression holding a kind of satisfaction. "So you *do* know about Mozambique?"

"You're not the only one with a re-con team, old man."

"What do you want? Why so much interest in my former researchers?"

"I told you," Evangela looked away quickly as if suddenly regretting how much she'd said. "I want a piece of the pie."

"Bull- you could buy and sell a small country a hundred times over by now. This isn't about money or vengeance. You want something specific from this so-called lab." He crossed his arms. "What?" his gaze shifted and then returned to her face. "More Re-Gen for Mae? It's useless, you know? Given her pre-existing-"

"I know that!" Eva snapped, rolling her eyes toward the ceiling. "I knew it'd be only a matter of time before she was useless to me. I've got more of that drug than I know what to do with. Mae popped them like peppermint. Everyone saw her taking them. They'd mistake her being high for being calm- everyone was happy. Unless she missed a dose…"

Jasper shook his head. "Already speaking of her in the past tense," he grinned. "The day may come when that poor…thing discovers how long you've been lying to her and about how much." His grin turned into a phony smile of reassurance when he saw Eva's eyes widen. "No dear,

Maeva hasn't joined your other crew members in the afterlife."

The news seemed to have a draining effect on Evangela who bowed her head as though defeated. "Get out," she moaned. "I promise not to go after your precious Belle."

"That's good," he squatted before her again. "The only reason you aren't dead now and didn't suffer back then was because I gave my word. But now you've threatened my child-my grandchild- all bets are off. Don't cross me on this Miss Ramsey. I *will* kill you but not before I share all of what I know with Maeva and I know a helluva lot.

"It'd be a god-awful mess to see her unraveled and unleashed with you in her sights." He stood. "I'll leave you to think on that and to get the place tidied up. Those bodies will start to stink in a while."

The sound of clunking boots, jingling knife blades and the gentle swish of material hit the air as Jasper Stone left the house with select members of his team in tow. They left the front door wide open, but to Eva it only appeared a blur through her tears fueled by malice and defeat. She slid to the floor, drawing the elegant chiffon folds of her white lounge dress about her as she tucked into a fetal position. All the while, she looked out into the night beyond the door.

Looming in the corridor, Maeva waited. Her feral gaze shadowed with concern and; for the first time ever, suspicion.

***

Carlos suffered another swat to the forehead. He'd been trying desperately not to laugh as his wife tried to assuage her cousin's fears during the phone call that had blessedly waited until after they'd enjoyed their third session of love making. They lay in an erotic entanglement of legs, arms and bed coverings.

Carlos nuzzled into Dena's soft belly while smiling his contentment. "Is she very angry?" He asked when the call ended with Sabra.

"I swear," Dena sighed. Without looking, she angled her arms over her head and set her mobile somewhere on the night table. "Smoak Tesano must have some kind of supernatural power over that girl. She was calm when we started talking, got riled up halfway through. I heard Smoak say something and then she was calm again. Like magic."

"Guess it's a good idea we let *him* tell her what's been happening over the last month." Carlos mused.

"Hmph, yeah," Lazily, Dena bumped her thigh against her husband's shoulder. "She wasn't too happy with Smoak's condensed version but when he suggested they elope, she was all good."

"Are you serious?" The news made Carlos lift his head.

Dena smiled. "Right now they're honeymooning somewhere in Tahiti."

"Good for them," Carlos' broad grin lent a more expressive sparkle to the pale yet all too captivating green of his stare.

"Hmph, for now," Dena cautioned. "They still have to tell Aunt Georgia."

Laughter colored the bedroom for a long time. Carlos fixed on a spot along Dena's hip for a while before he spoke.

"I want to ask you about the night I caught up to you and Nile in the parking lot with those guys."

The question gave Dena a start. "Okay," she managed to sound steady enough, recalling the night and the run in with Brogue Tesano's men.

"Why didn't you handle them?" Carlos asked. "From what I've seen, you could have."

Dena considered her response. "It was the last thing I expected and at first I just...just froze I think. They were leading me and Nile out of the hotel at gunpoint and all I could think about was how much like us she and Taurus were. So in love and about to be ruined because of secrets," sighing she absently raked her fingers across Carlos' close-cut hair. "The idea of it was so depressing and I-I couldn't make myself move." Her fingers drifted down to his cheek when he looked up.

"When you got there and *handled them*, it was like you'd *handled* the depression too and none of the rest mattered. We talked about what happened to me on the trip I took with Daddy and Marc but that was as much as I wanted to tell you and you never pressed for more even though you could have- should have."

Carlos drew her hand to his mouth, kissed it.

"I would've probably hidden out from telling the rest of the story forever had Mae and Eva not come knocking on our door and I knew I had as much unfinished business with them as with you."

236

Carlos rose up over his wife, his weight smothering Dena in a way she heartily enjoyed. The kiss they shared was long, heated and seeking.

"Your business with me isn't done yet, you know?" He questioned during their kiss.

Dena studied him curiously when he smiled down at her.

"I was wondering if I could get you to dismantle another gun for me?"

Dena burst into a fit of giggles. "Did you get some kind of sick joy out of that Mr. McPhereson?"

"Well, hell yeah but I didn't have time to fully appreciate it then, so I'd be grateful for a replay just to diagnose how sick I really am."

"I see," she linked her arms about his neck, "and is there anything else?"

"Hmm…oh yeah-be sure to overpower me."

Dena pushed him to his back, straddling his broad frame while she took a sensual inventory of his amazing physique.

"Aren't you a little nervous about what that might do to your fierce reputation?" She asked.

Carlos drew Dena down so that her curvy licorice-toned body draped him. "Not even a *little* bit." He swore and launched a hungry gnawing at her ear.

Dena Ramsey McPhereson's soft laughter was stirred by sheer desire and utter devotion to the love of her life.

~EPILOGUE~

"Fools!" Vale Tesano had never possessed the canyon deep voice octave that so many of his brothers could claim. Still, when he was riled, folks understood that it was in their best interests to be wary.

The man, to whom Vale was then frowning toward, stepped forward with raised hands. "Boss, I swear I'm right, I'd stake my life on it." Luke Baker said.

Vale tugged on the gleaming cuff links adorning his shirt. "That's good, 'cause you just have."

Though vastly outnumbered, SyBilla Ramsey fought valiantly against the restraints of the four men who held her. She had gained a small measure- a *very* small measure-of satisfaction over the fact that it had taken four of them to keep her planted on the chair. Her struggles sent the squeaks from the chair echoing into the bunker-style space each time she wrenched wildly against it.

Bill moved even more wildly when the man who'd been speaking to Vale Tesano moved closer to assist the man who held her thigh. When they spread her legs-letting her fears get the better of her, seemed imminent.

"Easy!" Vale hissed. "I don't want a mark on her."

Despite their wariness of their boss, the men looked at Vale like he'd just requested the impossible. Doing their best to be gentle, they eased Bill's bare legs apart. SyBilla had been asleep when she woke to find the men dragging her from bed and subsequently out of her home. They stowed her in a vehicle that seemed to drive for hours.

"There," Luke Baker announced in triumph.

Vale moved closer, frowning and then appearing stunned and then curious. At last, he lifted his dark gaze to SyBilla's hazy gray one.

"Where'd you get that?" He asked.

"Fuck you."

"That's no tattoo, is it love?"

"What do you know about it?" She spat.

Vale ran the back of his hand down her cheek. "I know those little black dots mark my property- property I've thrown away. So the questions now are how did *you* get one and more importantly, what are you doing alive Ms. Ramsey?"

A Lover's Debt

Dear Reader,

Carlos and Dena... like so many aspects of this series, I owe much to my awesome readers. So many of you asked, asked demanded *that I give the couple their own story. For a long time, I said there was no need- that their story was pretty much wrapped up in A Lover's Beauty and other books where they'd made an appearance.*

It seems that I was just as misled as Carlos and Dena for a while, huh? A few years ago when I made those claims that Dena's and Carlos' love story was complete I would never have suspected that anything as intricate as the previous tale would reside between them. Like you, I was thoroughly stunned when the details of this story unfolded for me.

I often talk about what a treat it is to create my heroes. Carlos was definitely no exception and I have to admit there were times when he gave me pause. There was an edge to him that made him grittier, disturbingly real- a man you wouldn't want to cross but a man whose appeal was undeniable.

The way Carlos got to me during the creation of this story is one of the things I love most about the cast of characters that comprise this series. I never know where they'll take me, but I know it'll be someplace riveting. Riveting- like the unexpected truth revealed about Michaela's father. The motivations behind Humphrey Tesano's research and the additional layers exposed about Eva and Mae Leer. This story was a real ride for me. I hope it was for you. Please do drop me a line to let me know what you think.

Up next, we find out SyBilla's fate and what challenges the upcoming events will pose for she and Caiphus in A Lover's Control.

Til next time,
Al
altonya@lovealtonya.com
www.lovealtonya.com
www.facebook.com/altonyaw
www.twitter.com/#!/ramseysgirl

THE RAMSEY/TESANO SERIES

A Lover's Dream
A Lover's Pretense
A Lover's Mask
A Lover's Regret
A Lover's Worth
A Lover's Beauty
A Lover's Soul
Lover's Allure
A Ramsey Wedding
Book of Scandal: The Ramsey Elders
Lover's Origin
A Lover's Shame
A Lover's Hate
A Lover's Sin
Vestige: A Ramsey Tesano Novella
Lover's Christmas
A Lover's Debt

An AlTonya Exclusive

A Lover's Debt

46038134R00146

Made in the USA
Middletown, DE
20 July 2017